FIVE ROADS TO
DEATH

FIVE ROADS TO DEATH

Judson Philips

A RED BADGE NOVEL OF SUSPENSE

DODD, MEAD & COMPANY
New York

1 2 3 4 5 6 7 8 9 10

Library of Congress Cataloging in Publication Data

Philips, Judson Pentecost, date
  Five roads to death.

  (A Red badge novel of suspense)
  I. Title.
PZ3.P5412Fi   [PS3531.H442]   813'.5'2   77–22467
ISBN 0–396–07472–3

PART ONE

1

He was stretched out in a sort of deck chair on the stone terrace in front of the cottage. The hot August sun beat down on his tanned face and arms, his eyes protected by a pair of black sunglasses. The girl, walking up the path toward him from where she had parked her car, thought he looked dark, handsome, romantic, like a man out of a Gothic novel. Perhaps that was because of what she knew about him, a man buried under a personal tragedy attempting to escape from grim realities. The girl was not religion oriented, but she prayed to whomever or whatever as she came closer to the man, prayed that she could find some way to get him to forget his own problems and interest himself in hers. She hadn't been given much hope by this man's friends, but she had to try.

She had a pleasant, free-swinging kind of walk, the man thought as he watched her approach, golden blonde hair that hung loosely down to her shoulders. She wore navy blue slacks and a blue man's shirt, open at the throat. Most women, he thought, didn't look well in slacks but this girl had the figure for them, thin hips and nicely tapered thighs and legs. Sometime, long ago in a dark past, he would have felt a natural male interest in her. Now he hoped she had simply lost her way and was coming to the first house she saw to ask for directions.

Instinct warned him that if she had lost her way it wasn't in a literal sense, and that she was coming to him for help he couldn't and wouldn't give.

He didn't move as she reached him and stood looking down at his long, lean figure in the deck chair.

"What can I do for you?" he asked.

"Peter Styles?"

"I suspect you know that," he said. "Who told you where you could find me, Miss—?"

"Lynn Mason," the girl said. "I understand there is only one person who could have told me where you were."

"Frank Devery?"

The girl nodded. She had very wide, candid blue eyes.

"The bastard," Peter Styles said, without anger.

Frank Devery was the publisher and managing editor of *Newsview* magazine, Peter Styles's boss and his closest friend. This cottage and the wooded area around it belonged to Devery. Peter Styles had come here to hide.

"I went to Mr. Devery for help," the girl said. "I wanted to find you and enlist you in a cause—my cause," Lynn Mason said.

"And Frank told you I was through with causes," Peter said. "Somehow you pried out of him that I was staying here in his cottage."

"You know Mr. Devery too well to believe anything could be pried out of him," the girl said. "He thought if you could be persuaded to listen to my story you just might—he said 'get up off your ass and rejoin the world.' "

"He was wrong," Peter said. He turned the black glasses away from the girl's face, which had grown tense with her need for something he had no intention of giving.

"I know your story, Mr. Styles," she said.

Who didn't know his story? Peter Styles, a top investigative reporter, devoted for a long time to fighting the terrorist forces

4

that grow stronger and more violent with the emerging of what is called "the Third World." The whole world knew that a few months ago Grace Styles, Peter's wife, had been assassinated by terrorists in a refugee camp for Vietnamese in California, a cold-blooded, pointless horror. Peter's fierce search for the people responsible had revealed a criminal conspiracy by a big multinational corporation and at the same time wiped out the terrorist group responsible for his wife's death. He was, briefly, a hero who wanted no medals, only some merciful blackout from memories too bitter to endure. He had taken what was called a "leave of absence" from *Newsview*. "Going to write a book," Devery told inquiring friends. But Peter wasn't writing a book, wasn't trying to write a book or thinking about it. He wanted to forget and he hadn't found a way.

"There is a guy I love maybe as much as you loved your wife, Mr. Styles," Lynn Mason said. "We believe he is alive, but for how long? He is in the hands of terrorists as vicious and as evil as the people who murdered your wife. The government won't help my guy; the company for which he works can't help him; the media won't help him."

Peter Styles was trained to listen. In spite of his instinct to resist he had listened to the girl.

"The media?" he asked.

"The newspapers, the news magazines like *Newsview,* the television and radio."

"In what way could the media help him?"

"Publicizing his story, creating a public outrage that would force governments and his business to act." Her voice was going defiant, with a kind of passionate intensity.

"So why won't the media stir up a storm?" Peter asked.

"Because—because they depend on their advertising. Because Big Business—in capital letters—doesn't want a storm stirred up."

"That may be true in some cases," Peter said. "About the

media, I mean. But if you talked to Frank Devery you know his advertisers could go fly a kite if they suggested he cover up on a genuine news story."

"And yet he won't print this story," Lynn Mason said, "unless you, Peter Styles, convince him that it's safe to print it."

A tight little smile moved the corners of Peter's mouth. Devery was playing games. He had come up with a gimmick to get Peter to come out of hiding and interest himself in something.

"I'm afraid I'm not your man, Lynn," he said.

She looked as though she hadn't heard. Very young, he thought. "Do you remember the kidnapping of Richard Potter?" she asked. "It happened some time before—before your own tragedy, Peter."

First names had come easy. Richard Potter? He remembered vaguely—some political shenanigans in South America; an executive of a big United States corporation held for ransom, political prisoners to be released, money to the poor—other things he couldn't remember.

"That was a long time ago," he said.

"Four months and thirteen days," she said.

Too much horror had been crowded into that space of time for him to remember any details about the Potter case. "The kidnappers' demands haven't been met?"

"Haven't been met, and have been doubled since they were originally made. Somebody screwed up. One of the terrorist leaders was killed during an attempted negotiation."

"Killed by whom?"

"The Carrados police."

"Then the government at Carrados was trying to negotiate?"

"I don't think it was for real. I think they were only trying to locate the terrorists' headquarters."

Peter reached into his shirt pocket for a cigarette. Almost as an afterthought he passed the pack to Lynn. She took one. He

6

held his lighter for her and then lit his own. He didn't want any part of it. He didn't want to move from this cottage, this deck chair, for a long, long time. He didn't want to go back to the wars.

"Four months is a long time," he said. "How do you know your Richard Potter is still alive?"

"I know for certain he was alive a week ago," Lynn said. "Then the terrorists' leader was murdered by the police. Whether they have retaliated—" Her lips trembled.

"How do you know he was alive a week ago? Because they said so?"

She shook her head. "The chief of security in Carrados, a man named Manuel Carbo, demanded proof that Dick was alive before he would negotiate. He insisted on talking to Dick on the telephone. The terrorists refused. They came up with a solution. They would prepare four questions for Dick that only he could answer. Questions of an intimate and personal nature. Two of those questions were prepared by his wife, two by people on his staff at Harkness Chemical. The man who was later murdered by the Carrados police came back with the right answers to those questions. Only Dick could have supplied those answers. He was alive."

"Hold on a minute," Peter said. He sat up a little straighter in his deck chair. "You spoke of a man you loved as much as I loved my wife. You called him 'my guy.' Now you mention his wife."

"Is it inconceivable that I could be in love with another woman's husband?"

"I suppose not." He leaned back again in his chair. "Now I imagine you will tell me that Devery has agreed to give me the assignment and you want me to go to Carrados, in South America, to find your man?"

"No."

"Well, that's something."

7

"Because I know Dick isn't in South America."

"That's where he was kidnapped, wasn't it?"

"Yes. But he isn't there now."

"How do you know?"

"Let me tell you about the four questions," Lynn said. "First there were two from Frances, Dick's wife. She asked: 'What were we discussing in a suite at the Hotel Beaumont on an evening in April of this year?' His answer was: 'We were discussing a divorce.' Nobody else could have known that but Dick. Her second question was: 'Are there any distinguishing marks or scars on my body?' His answer was: 'You have a very small, pale blue birthmark on the inside of your right thigh.' Then came a question from Sam Evans, Dick's top assistant at Harkness Chemical. 'What was your golf score the last time we played?' The answer was: 'Seventy-seven.' It was memorable because it was the lowest score Dick had ever made. The final question came from me. Sam Evans came to me for it. It was a trick question. I asked: 'What were you concerned about just before you left for Carrados?' Dick's answer was: 'I was concerned about us.' That's how I know he isn't in South America."

"I don't follow."

"I told you it was a trick question," Lynn said.

"Nice of him to be concerned about you in the midst of his troubles."

"Please, Peter, listen!" She sat down on the stone wall next to his deck chair, her eyes narrowed against the smoke from her cigarette. "Dick Potter's job at Harkness Chemical is very special. He has the title of vice-president, but actually he is a sort of diplomatic trouble shooter. It's no secret that the big multinational corporations have under-the-table dealings with all kinds of people in foreign countries—politicians, diplomats, rich businessmen, and men who want to get rich through business. Most of these dealings are off the record. Dick's areas of operation were in Latin America, the Middle East, Europe, and of course here in the United States. He would take off without any word as to where he was going. He just wouldn't turn up at the office one morning and no one would have any idea where he was. He and I invented a system whereby he would get a message to me that would tell me, in a broad sense, where he was. He would get word to me that 'I am concerned about Sam.' Sam Evans, as I told you, is his assistant. But being concerned about Sam meant he was in South America. S.A.—the first two letters. 'I am concerned about you' meant Europe—you, Europe. 'I am concerned about me,' meant the Middle East— me, Middle East. 'I am concerned about us' meant the United States—us, United States. His answer to my question means that he is in the United States. 'I was concerned about us' is his way of telling me that he is in the United States."

"The Harkness people know that?" Peter asked.

"It wasn't a company code, Peter. It was just something between Dick and me. If I knew in a general way where he was I could tell pretty accurately where, in that part of the world, he was likely to be."

"But you've told the company—the people who need to know—that he's probably somewhere in the United States?"

"I've told them, but the people who might do something don't seem to take it too seriously. In any case it's not specific enough to do much good."

"You said if you knew the general area where he was you could tell pretty accurately where, in that general area, he might be."

"Not in this case," she said. "All it tells me is that he isn't where everyone thinks he is—somewhere in South America."

Peter crushed out his cigarette in the glass ashtray on the little table beside his deck chair. Damn the woman, she had stirred his interest.

"Do we know for certain that he was kidnapped in South

9

America?" he asked.

"Yes."

"But if he is here doesn't that suggest he may never have left this country?"

"Oh, he left the country. He was flown to Carrados in one of the Harkness Chemical private jets. The pilot, the copilot, and the stewardess saw him walk across the airstrip into the flight terminal. That's the last any of his friends saw of him. Hours later the demands came from the terrorists."

Peter shook his head. "Why would the kidnappers fly him back to this country?"

"I don't have the faintest idea," Lynn said. "But he's here. I know that."

In spite of himself Peter was interested. The girl was so young, so sure of herself. "How did you get to ask one of the four questions?"

"Sam Evans, Dick's assistant, came to me. They wanted questions nobody could research. So I supplied Sam with the code question. 'What were you concerned about when you left for Carrados?' "

"Why would Evans come to you?"

"Because I'm Dick's girl."

"You mean his mistress."

"How old-fashioned can you get, Peter? I love him. He loves me. We spend whatever time we can together. He isn't 'keeping' me, if that's what you're asking."

"How did it happen? You work in his company?"

"No. I—I'm an entertainer. Folk singer. I work in a nightspot in the Village. Dick came there one night. He offered to buy me a drink after I'd done my thing. It happened that night, just like that. We knew then it was forever."

"But he stays married?"

"Yes. My life story isn't very important, Peter. Finding Dick is all that matters."

Peter drew a deep breath and let it out slowly. He was hooked.

"Care for some coffee?" he asked.

Frank Devery's apartment on Beekman Place in New York was only slightly less austere than his office in the *Newsview* building. Under the handicap of a chaotic disorder in both places cleaning women cleaned, but not a single sheet of manuscript, not a newspaper or magazine clipping, not a reel of tape or film must be touched on pain of death. The helter-skelter scattering of things seemed totally disorganized, yet Devery could reach out and locate anything he wanted without hesitation.

Devery was a short, stocky man with sandy brown hair and bright blue inquisitive eyes. Outsiders thought of him as an abrasive, slave-driving kind of a man, but people who knew him and worked for him knew that beneath the surface was compassion for people and that he would go all the way out to the end of the limb for his "family." Being a bachelor, his "family" were the people who worked for him at *Newsview,* from Peter Styles, his top man and closest friend, down to the newest and lowest-ranking copy boy in the printing plant. He was a fighter for justice as well as for friends. Somebody had made an affectionate quip about him at the office, based on a television commercial. "We don't have a piece of the rock here at *Newsview.* We have the rock itself."

It was after midnight that August night—or early morning —and Devery had just finished reading the flimsies for that week's edition of *Newsview.* The flimsies are the typewritten copies of everything that would be set up in print tomorrow. Nothing, even three lines of meaningless filler, went into print without Devery's approving initials on the flimsies. That was how tight a hold he had on the content of his magazine. He was not a nit-picking editor. People writing "opinion" had a free

11

hand, even though Devery might disagree with them violently. Books, movies, music, the arts—Devery never interfered with a reviewer's comments. He did make decisions about major stories, whether to feature them or not. In the end, after he had read the flimsies on a Monday night, he was ready for any kind of outside criticism or attack. *"I know every damn word that's in my magazine and I stand ready to defend all of them!"*

That early Tuesday morning—shortly after midnight—Devery was headed for the sideboard in the living room to pour himself a double bourbon. It was the first of the night. He never drank on Monday nights until the last flimsy had been read and approved. He looked forward to a hefty slug when he was done. It helped him unwind. He had just put two ice cubes into an oversized old-fashion glass when his doorbell rang. He swore softly, withdrew his hand from the bottle of bourbon, and went to the door.

Peter Styles stood there. He was wearing light tan slacks, a summer-weight corduroy jacket, a navy blue sport shirt. There were dark circles under his eyes. He looked tired.

"You finished?" he asked. He knew Devery's schedule.

"Your timing is perfect," Devery said. "Double or triple bourbon?"

"A single will do for now," Peter said. He also knew this apartment as well as he knew his own on Irving Place. He sat down in an armchair beside Devery's littered flat-top desk. For a moment he lowered his head and pressed the tips of his fingers against his closed eyelids. Devery came over from the sideboard and handed his friend a drink. He didn't have to ask how much water to add to the two ounces of whiskey he considered a single drink. He knew from years of pouring.

"You are a sonofabitch, you know," Peter said.

Devery hefted his four-ounce double. "Shall we drink to the lady who seems to have got to you?"

"So you had your way," Peter said. "Okay, I'll drink to her.

12

But I have questions, chum."

"Shoot." Devery shoved some papers aside and sat down on the corner of his desk.

"Why not?" Peter asked.

"Why not what?"

"Why isn't the magazine blowing the roof off the Potter kidnapping?"

"The man's life is at stake," Devery said. His face had taken on the hard, set look Peter recognized as his fighting mask.

"It's been at stake for four months and thirteen days—fourteen days as of this morning. We know he was alive at least a week ago. Nobody is lifting a finger to help him, except some bungling security people in Carrados who killed a man trying to get him to talk. Now the terrorists have doubled their demands and Potter, if he is still alive, is in real big trouble. And you sit here on your behind doing nothing about it."

"I sent Lynn Mason to see you," Devery said quietly.

"Come on, chum! Are you telling me I'm the person to help him? This isn't some suspense writer's cook-up, you know. This is the real world. Governments are involved. Big business is involved. The terrorists who are trying to take over the world everywhere are involved. One miserable investigative reporter doesn't find answers for all that."

"Lynn Mason tell you what the terrorists' demands were—and are?" Devery asked.

Peter ticked them off on his fingers. "Five hundred political prisoners to be released. A bonus of a year's salary to all Latin Americans working for Harkness Chemical in Carrados. Food packages for ten thousand destitute citizens living in Carrados. Terrorist propaganda to be printed in the local press and broadcast over the television and radio stations."

Devery nodded. "And now everything doubled, thanks to police bungling."

"And you don't think this is a story worth shouting from the

13

rooftops? You don't think so, nor do any other newspapers or news magazines, nor do any of our radio or television networks after the first demands were made. What the hell is this, Frank? Harkness Chemical carries ads in *Newsview*. Did they buy you off?"

"Don't talk like a horse's ass!" Devery said, a little muscle twitching along the line of his jaw.

"All right, Frank, let me have it," Peter said.

Pent-up anger was in the sound of Devery's voice. "Fact one," he said. "Four months and fourteen days ago—your figures—Potter was flown to Carrados in a Harkness Chemical private jet. What he was going there for I don't know and it doesn't matter. The pilot of that plane was a man named Weldon Keach, a minor executive of Harkness. He flew bombers in Vietnam. He is an old and close friend of Potter's. He often flew the company planes because he likes to fly. There was a copilot, hired simply as a pilot by the company, and a stewardess, also hired by the company for just that job. They landed Potter at the airport in Carrados, saw him walk across the airstrip and into the flight terminal. That was that. No one who knows Potter has seen him since."

"That Lynn told me," Peter said.

"Fact two," Devery said. "Some four hours later Harkness Chemical got demands from the terrorists. Political prisoners, bonuses, food packages, propaganda. It represented about three million bucks to Harkness Chemical."

"That much?"

"That much." Devery reached for a cigar on his desk but he didn't light it. "Fact three. The executive director of Harkness's operations in Carrados was a man named Wilfred Hadley. He is a decent guy and he responded in decent terms. He would pay the bonuses. He would either supply the food packages or contribute an equivalent sum of money to the local people for distribution among the Carrados poor. He would see to it that

14

the terrorists' propaganda was aired in the local press and over the broadcasting stations. He could not do anything about political prisoners, but he would pass that demand on to the very top, President Luis Perrault."

"And His Excellency, the President, wouldn't play along?"

"It took him two days to decide that he wouldn't play along," Devery said. "Meanwhile Hadley didn't wait. He passed out the bonuses to three hundred workers. He put a huge sum of money in escrow for the local poor. He had to have approval from higher up to get that kind of money. So far Harkness was doing everything they could to get Potter back. Hadley then carried the terrorists' propaganda to the local newspapers and the radio and TV stations. Here he ran into trouble. No one would print or broadcast that material without approval from the government. Hadley was determined to live up to his end of the bargain. He went next door."

"Meaning?"

"Neighboring countries. Their TV and radio stations reach Carrados easily, even their newspapers are circulated. It was the best Hadley could do to live up to his end of the bargain. Then, two days later, President Perrault threw the book at him."

"How?"

"The government would not deal with terrorists. They would meet no demands, make no concessions, and anyone who did was in big trouble. Their position on Richard Potter was the same as Israel's had been over the hostages at Entebbe. No deal. Now it gets sticky."

"Hadley was in the soup?"

"The big soup. Carrados is, it says here, a democracy. The neighbors who printed and broadcast the propaganda are not. They sympathize with the terrorists' revolutionary programs. They were supported quite openly by Cuba and other communist-dominated countries. Perrault took the stand that if he

15

gave in to the terrorists it would make his government look so weak it might be overthrown. It may be a good stand. It was Israel's stand. It is the position our own government takes. No deal with terrorists, hijackers, kidnappers. But Perrault went further—and here I think he wasn't motivated by political wisdom, political courage, but by political greed."

"In what way?"

"Anyone who violated the government stand would be punished," Devery said. "Harkness Chemical had violated that stand, even though they acted two days before the government made its position clear. The punishment, the government announced, was expropriation."

"Meaning exactly?"

"The government would take over Harkness Chemical's assets in Carrados—'at a fair price' is, I believe, the phrase. The government, not Harkness, determines what is a fair price, and Harkness has no redress. Now, Harkness had been willing to pay out three million dollars to get Richard Potter back. Fair? Generous? But now we're talking about something approaching a hundred million, with annual profits of God knows how many millions. Is one man's life worth that much?"

"So that's it!" Peter said, softly.

"Not only is Harkness Chemical concerned, but so are dozens of other multinational corporations in Latin America. If Perrault and the Carrados government can get away with this 'for cause,' causes can be invented for taking over billions of dollars worth of United States investments. There is already so much anti–United States feeling in Latin America that adherents of democracy can do little to quiet it. Perrault's position with his own people is strengthened by his taking a tough stand against Harkness. The other multinationals, banded together in an organization called Council of the Americas, have got to find a way around this. So, to start with, Harkness has to change its position. No bonuses, no money for food for the poor, no releases to the media. Wilfred Hadley is fired for being trigger-happy. Our State Department brings quiet pressure on Perrault, but they daren't make him look bad. Harkness must play it Perrault's way, and hope he relents."

"So Richard Potter becomes the forgotten man."

Devery bit down hard on his unlighted cigar. "It might be more realistic to say that Richard Potter is a dead man. The terrorists can't afford to let themselves look weak any more than Perrault can. So, if they don't get their way, Potter will be killed. I believe he's still alive because I think that when he's killed it will be done in a flamboyant way for the whole revolutionary movement to see."

"And you won't fight it in print?"

"The State Department has urged us, politely, to lay off while they try their own undercover methods. If we get into the act, print the story as I've told it to you, and Potter is murdered—well, the media will be accused of being unconcerned about a man's life for the sake of a sensational story. So help me, Peter, if I thought going to bat, out in front, would save Potter, I'd go, and damn the torpedoes. I'm afraid I don't believe that kind of heroics will help him."

"So we just sit by and wait for the terrorists to deliver us Potter's head on a silver platter."

"I didn't say sit by," Devery said. He looked steadily at Peter. "I said I wouldn't go into print with the story. I didn't say I wouldn't dig. I didn't say I wouldn't try to find Potter. I didn't say that after Potter is dead I wouldn't blow these bastards off the face of the earth in print, with every detail we can get."

Peter put down his emptied glass on the edge of the desk. Devery took it and walked over to the sideboard for a refill.

"What do you make of Lynn Mason's conviction that Potter is being held somewhere back in this country? 'I was concerned about us'—us, United States."

17

"She believes it."

"Why would they fly him back to the United States?"

Devery brought back the fresh drink. "Perhaps because everybody—the Perrault government, Harkness, probably the CIA, agents for the multinationals—will be looking for him in Carrados. Moving him out would minimize their risks."

"It's hard to know where to start," Peter said.

"I can give you a list of names of people who might be useful," Devery said. He sounded quite casual. "If you're willing—"

Peter gave him a bitter little smile. "I'm willing," he said.

2

What would you like to be when you grow up? A policeman? A fireman? That's how it begins, and through your adolescence and school and college days you finally decide on something real. If you are lucky and good at it you make it.

Peter Styles had wanted to be a writer, and he had made it early. Not long after college he had begun to develop a reputation as a witty observer and commentator on life's absurdities. He wrote much-quoted pieces for *Newsview*, *The New Yorker*, and other sophisticated publications. He was a familiar figure at gatherings of famous and talked-about people in the theater, the arts. He had a life-style that pleased him.

And then one winter, driving home from a ski resort in Vermont, he had been driven off the road by some hopped-up kids, his car somersaulting down a mountainside. He had come to in a hospital in a Vermont town with his right leg amputated below the knee.

His world changed after that. He was no longer the bright, witty young man about town. He was obsessed by an almost paranoid need to find the two boys responsible for his mutilation in order to punish them. An eye for an eye, a leg for a leg! He never came on the track of the boys, but he found himself involved in a one-man crusade against the senseless violence that seemed to be engulfing the world. Socially he withdrew, self-conscious about the limp that even a marvelously constructed artificial leg and foot couldn't hide entirely. He avoided women. He would be repulsive to them, he thought.

Then Grace came into his life, Grace, dark, vibrant, excitingly alive. They were instantly so much in love that nothing else in the world mattered. He was restored to complete manhood again. His crusade against violence lost its tinge of personal revenge. Grace shared it with him. For five incredible years they shared a life, were a perfect One.

Then, for the second time, Peter's life was shattered by senseless violence—Grace's brutal murder by a group of terrorists in California. Grief and rage and a passionate thirst for revenge drove Peter to the total destruction of that particular group. After that there was nothing to live for. He had sat for weeks in Devery's country house trying, without success, to find some reason for living at all.

Then a blonde girl had walked up the path to Devery's cottage and dumped something in his lap. A decent man was being used like a poker chip in a grab game for power. The instinct to help, to fight a familiar evil, was, he found, still strong in him. He wanted no part of it but he couldn't resist it. A human life used as a bargaining piece offended him.

It was about two-thirty in the morning when Peter left Devery's apartment on Beekman Place. Upper windows in the giant apartment houses were dark. Most of the city was asleep. Peter was very much awake after weeks of being in something like an emotional coma. Time had to be used. If it wasn't already too late to do anything for Richard Potter, an hour from now, a day from now, might be.

One of Peter's good friends was Lieutenant Gregory Maxvil of Manhattan Homicide. Maxvil was a trim, steel-wire kind of man with penetrating dark eyes that appeared able to read the label on the inside of your shirt collar. Maxvil was the new

20

breed of cop, with a law degree and a complete knowledge of all the scientific techniques of crime fighting. He was also a cop who cultivated contacts outside his own city, for New York with the United Nations is, in a sense, the capital of the world. Peter had always said if you wanted to reach someone in Timbuctoo all you had to do was ask Maxvil and he would tell you instantly who to locate and how to locate him—or her. Maxvil's beat was the world of crime even though his jurisdiction was the borough of Manhattan in New York City. Sooner or later, Maxvil believed, the big fish were bound to come his way.

Maxvil's apartment was only a few blocks south of Devery's. Shortly before three in the morning he answered an imperative ringing of his doorbell. He slept in the raw and he had pulled on a blue terrycloth robe, was barefoot, and angry—until he saw Peter.

"Welcome back to the human race," he said. "Come in. It's not a respectable time of night, but come in."

"I need help," Peter said.

"I didn't suppose you'd come here to show me colored slides of your vacation from living," Maxvil said. It was a tough way to deal with Peter's tragedy, but probably the right way.

Peter went into the familiar living room with its nice collection of paintings by artists who were personal friends of the detective.

"If it's a long story I'll make drinks," Maxvil said.

"It's long and complicated."

Maxvil disappeared for a moment and returned wearing a pair of slacks and bedroom slippers under his robe. He produced two drinks, a package of cigarettes, and sat down facing Peter. He was a good listener, Peter knew. There would be no questions until Peter came to the end of what he had to tell, unless Maxvil needed something to keep the story straight in his mind.

When Peter finished Richard Potter's story Maxvil had

21

poured a second drink and smoked five cigarettes without speaking a word. Maxvil lit his sixth cigarette and leaned back in his overstuffed armchair.

"Your friend Potter seems poised at a crossroads facing five different roads to death," he said. "The terrorists will almost certainly kill him unless you can find him and drag him away. That's one road. The Carrados government may kill him, indirectly, through bungling. Harkness Chemical by deciding that their profits are more important than a man's life may bring it about. Uncle Sam himself, with his subtle pressures to keep Carrados in the democratic fold, may be responsible. Finally your people, the media, can send him down the skids by blowing up the story too soon and too colorfully. Five roads to death."

"Potter can only die once," Peter said. "It can't make much difference to him who is responsible."

"The point is, can everybody's shirt be kept on for a while till you can find Potter?"

Peter sat forward. "Are you saying you think one man can go up against two governments, a revolutionary army, and a multinational corporation and free a hostage they all want?"

"If you didn't think so, you wouldn't be here, would you?" Maxvil asked. "How can I help?"

"It's a crazy idea!"

"One man can sometimes get through a hole in the fence when an army can't," Maxvil said.

"So where is the fence?" Peter reached for one of Maxvil's cigarettes. "That's where you can help me, Greg. I have to take the Mason girl's story seriously. Potter was flown back to this country. He was able to convey that through a trick question among the four asked him to make sure he is still alive. Where would they hide him here?"

Maxvil gave his friend a tight little smile. "New York, Chicago, San Francisco, Dallas. What's the old saying? 'Where would you hide a leaf? In a forest.' You hide an important man where there are crowds of people. The people holding him may be, probably are, Spanish speaking. So, Spanish Harlem, the Puerto Rican section here in New York. Personally I would like Dallas if I was hiding him. Close to the Mexican border if I had to move him in a hurry."

"Needle in a haystack," Peter said, "and you don't even have a hint which haystack."

"But all over this country—all over the world for that matter —there are ears that listen," Maxvil said. "Most of those listening ears will talk for a price."

"Money?"

Maxvil shook his head. "Information in return for information, immunity from prosecution, perhaps for a friend, a betrayal for a betrayal. I can pass the word and wait for someone to answer."

Peter brought his fist down on the arm of his chair. "There is no time! Tomorrow may be too late."

"Sometimes you catch a fish the first time you cast," Maxvil said. "Sometimes you can fish for a week with all the fancy lures in your bait box and never get a bite. You have to try. You know something, Peter?"

"Very little."

"That's the trouble. You know too damn little about the man you're looking for. Why was he chosen by the terrorists as a hostage? Why would they assume Harkness Chemical and President Perrault would pay such a big price for him? Why not the president of Harkness, or a political figure of importance? There has to be a reason for choosing Potter, a reason they would assume might make the company and the government go to such lengths to get him back."

"I can't begin to guess," Peter said.

Maxvil shrugged. "Maybe he knows something about Harkness that would hurt if he talked. Maybe he knows something about Harkness's dealings with the Carrados government that would hurt if he talked. He isn't just meat on the hoof, Peter. He was chosen as a hostage because he is who he is. But who is he?"

"And I find that out in a few hours, a day or two?"

"You're a professional fact finder," Maxvil said. "One thing sticks out for me. The man who was in charge at Harkness in Carrados—is it Wilfred Hadley?—he didn't wait a minute to respond to the terrorists' demands. He paid the bonuses, he got up the money for food packages, he arranged to have the terrorists' propaganda broadcast and printed. No hesitation. Potter was worth a huge price. If the terrorists had taken a men's room attendant out of the Harkness office building, would the answer have been the same? You can bet against it. There would have been cries of outrage, but no dough on the line, no risks run. Your girl friend says Hadley acted like a decent man. That's baloney. Hadley acted like a man who knew exactly what Potter was worth to Harkness. This Hadley could tell you that, Peter, if you could find him. He was fired, you say. He may be back in this country."

"I suppose someone in the Harkness office here in New York could tell me in the morning." He glanced at his watch. "Four or five hours from now."

"You going to waste the rest of the night?" Maxvil asked. "Can you locate your Miss Mason? She may know where Hadley is. She might also be able to tell you the right Harkness executives to get up in the middle of the night if Hadley isn't available. You said it, Peter, remember? Time is the enemy. You can't sit around theorizing. Meanwhile I'll blow some seductive music in the direction of the listening ears I know about. Who knows? We might get lucky."

Peter had needed Maxvil to tell him he wasn't an idiot to go

24

up against such impossible odds.

Four o'clock in the morning.

Lynn Mason didn't answer her home telephone. Peter recalled that she'd said the place where she worked, the Greenwich Corner, was a kind of all-night club. He found the address in the Manhattan telephone directory and took a cab there.

It wasn't wide open. Someone peered out at him through the grillwork in the top panel of a heavy door at street level. He was informed that the place was closed.

"I'm a friend of Lynn Mason's," Peter said. He gave his name when asked.

He was left standing on the street for a good five minutes before the door was opened by a thickset bouncer type.

"She's on at the moment, but she'll see you after," the man said.

It was a not unattractive room. There were heavy beams in the ceiling, dark red drapes at the windows. A caricaturist had decorated the walls with impudent and witty drawings of local and national celebrities. The lighting was muted, except for a single spot that was focused on Lynn Mason's golden head. She was seated on a sort of bar stool on a platform against the far wall. She played a guitar and sang in a clear, small voice. She wore blue jeans and a man's shirt, just as he had seen her the first time the morning before. Country music was not Peter's dish but he recognized that Lynn was much better than ordinary. There were perhaps a couple of dozen people scattered at tables around the room. They listened, pleased. Lynn knew how to hold her audience. Peter understood how Richard Potter could have been captivated by this girl. She was attractive offstage. There was something magical about her in performance.

She finished her number and instantly some of the people crowded around her. She had spotted Peter at the table where

25

the bouncer type had placed him and she made her excuses.

"Perhaps I shouldn't have come here," Peter said as she joined him.

"That was it for tonight," she said. "Did you—did you like it at all?"

"Enough to want to hear a lot more."

She leaned forward. "Is there something, Peter?"

"A little motion from a couple of friends," Peter said.

A waitress approached the table.

"A Virgin Mary," Lynn said.

"What's that?" Peter asked.

"A Bloody Mary without the vodka," Lynn said. "You?"

"A bourbon on the rocks," Peter said. "Can we talk here?"

"I have to stay a bit longer. I have to do a goodnight number."

"I've talked to a wise friend, a cop who may be helpful," Peter said. "He suggested there was a special reason for the terrorists choosing your Richard Potter as a hostage, a reason why Wilfred Hadley didn't hesitate to meet their demands instantly."

"A man's life was at stake!" Lynn said.

"Not good enough. Potter's life was worth three million bucks without Hadley even trying to negotitate. What made Potter so valuable to Harkness Chemical?"

She sat very still, frowning. He thought she looked like a little girl puzzling over some school problem. The waitress brought their drinks.

"You were his girl," Peter said. "He must have talked to you about his job. What made him so important?"

She reached out for her seasoned tomato juice, but she didn't lift the glass. "You must know something about the way the big multinationals operate," she said. "You—you've had experience with them."

Such bitter experience, he could have said. A big corporation

26

had been, callously, behind the murder of his wife.

"The public image is business out in the open," she said. "The private functioning is so often under the table. The Lockheed bribes? Express outrage about it and they'll tell you that's the way business has always been done with foreign powers. You buy orders and favors under the table."

"Wheeling and dealing is Potter's job?"

"Yes."

"So you know what he was wheeling and dealing for in Carrados?"

"No."

He waited for her to go on.

"I—I am what matters to Dick outside his job," she said. "Very early on he made it clear he didn't want to talk about his job. Early on he told me it wouldn't be safe for me to know his business secrets. He shared only one secret with me."

"And that was?"

She lowered her eyes. "That he loves me," she said. "I didn't know, for example, that he was going to Carrados. 'I won't see you tomorrow,' was all he said. It was understood that I wouldn't ask why, or where he would be. He said more than once that if I didn't know where he was going I couldn't tell anyone who might ask me."

"But you had your little code so he could give you an idea."

"If he had to stay away longer than usual," Lynn said.

"But you have no idea why he went to Carrados this time, or what made the terrorists think Harkness Chemical would go out on the limb for him?"

"I thought Wilfred Hadley was just protecting one of his people."

"I understand Hadley was fired. Do you have any idea where he is?"

"As a matter of fact I do," Lynn said. "He's staying in Sam Evans's apartment, not very far from here in the Village."

27

"Evans is Potter's assistant?"

"Sam told me," Lynn said. "Sam knew about Dick and me. I guess Dick needed to talk to someone when he was away. Sam is a good friend. He went to Carrados a few days ago to find some trace of Dick. Poor Sam, he insists on blaming himself for what happened to Dick."

"Oh?"

"He was supposed to make the trip with Dick in the company jet. He slept through the departure time. He slept through a phone call Dick made from the airport—according to Weldon Keach, the pilot. Dick was naturally concerned. Sam insists someone must have slipped him a Mickey at a party he attended the night before. He thinks if he had been with Dick he might have protected him from the kidnappers."

"Could we try to reach Hadley? He's got answers, you know."

"We can call Sam's number," she said.

They went to a phone booth in a far corner. She had a small address book in her purse and she found the number and dialed it. She frowned at the phone. "Temporarily out of order," she said.

"If it's close by let's go find him," Peter said.

"I have to do my last number." She smiled at him. "Is there anything you'd particularly like?"

"I'm afraid I'm not too familiar with your kind of thing, Lynn."

"I'll try one of my own on you," she said.

She went back to her stool on the platform. The little spotlight came on and illuminated her gold hair. She picked up her guitar and struck a chord. The room was instantly silent.

"To say goodnight I'd like to sing you a song of my own," she announced, "dedicated to a missing friend."

She went into a sad, minor key little ballad called "Little Boy Lost." There may have been others beside Peter in the audience

28

who knew she was thinking of Richard Potter as she sang. It was touching and very well done.

When she finished there was applause and goodnights and presently Peter and Lynn walked out into the pale dawn light and started walking along Greenwich Avenue toward Sam Evans's apartment.

A red fire chief's car swept past them, siren wailing.

Lynn looked up at Peter. She had a nice, brisk way of walking, keeping pace with him stride for stride. "You like?" she asked.

"I liked it fine," he said. "Has Potter heard it? It's for him, isn't it?"

"He wasn't lost the last time I saw him," she said, looking straight ahead.

They turned a corner and Lynn's fingers closed tightly on Peter's wrist. Ahead of them the street was crowded with fire equipment. Streams of water were being pumped at the roof level of a five-story dwelling. People had crowded into the street outside, some of them in nightclothes.

"That's Sam's building," Lynn said. "His apartment is the penthouse. On the roof!"

The sidewalk had been roped off and a fireman blocked their approach. Peter produced his press card and the fireman was willing to talk.

"Fire's in the penthouse," he said. "It's under control now, but too late for the poor bastard who lives there."

"Smoke?" Peter asked.

"Worse than that. The body's charred beyond recognition. The landlady says the regular tenant loaned the place to a friend. Friend must have been smoking in bed, gone to sleep. Place is gutted."

Lynn's fingernails bit into the flesh of Peter's wrist.

"We were coming to see him," she said.

The fireman's face was grim. "You won't want to see him.

29

About the only way they'll be able to identify him is by dental charts."

A fire captain took information from them. They believed the dead man might be one Wilfred Hadley. Lynn knew that Hadley originated from somewhere in the midwest, but he had been living in Carrados for the last seven or eight years. He was a bachelor as far as she knew, and she had no information about any family or nearest of kin. Records at Harkness Chemical's employment department would provide all that—if the man who had burned to death was Hadley.

They walked away, finally, leaving addresses with the authorities.

"How awful for him, and what bad luck for us," Lynn said.

Peter looked down at her. "Luck?" he said, in a flat voice.

"Peter!" She stopped walking.

"When you've been in my business as long as I have," Peter said, "you distrust anything that's labeled 'bad luck' or 'coincidence.' Hadley could have told us why Potter was picked by the terrorists as a hostage, why he had believed Harkness would pay anything to get him back. He'd been fired, made the fall guy in the eyes of the Perrault government in Carrados. He was probably outraged and ready to talk to us—or someone."

"What he knew somebody else in Harkness knows," Lynn said.

"But somebody else isn't going to talk," Peter said. "There's a new game plan, obviously." There was a sidewalk phone booth just ahead. "I want to talk to Maxvil."

The detective sounded wide awake as Peter gave him the latest.

"There'll be an autopsy, won't there, Greg?"

"Routine," Maxvil said.

"Can you interest yourself in it?"

"The autopsy? Yes. You think—"

"That someone may have wanted to keep him from talking," Peter said.

"You think the fire might have been an afterthought?"

"It could hide a violence, couldn't it?"

"I'll be in touch," Maxvil said.

If Harkness Chemical knew why the terrorists had chosen Richard Potter as a hostage, and had backed off from helping him because of the threat of expropriation by the Carrados government, Peter knew there was no point in talking to higher-ups in the corporation. They meant to keep the facts buried, if Peter's hunch about Wilfred Hadley's death was correct.

Lynn's apartment was on Jane Street, not far away. They walked there, neither of them talking. The apartment was up one flight in an old-fashioned residence building, a living room, bedroom, kitchenette, and bath. Nothing about it suggested that an important executive at Harkness Chemical had contributed to it. The furnishing was simple, comfortable. The walls of the living room were decorated with a few posters advertising appearances Lynn had made at different places, one or two professional photographs of her in action, and auto-graphed pictures of other performers who had probably played on the same bill with her. There was a little spinet piano in one corner, a guitar resting on top of it. The girl lived here, worked here. Peter wondered if perhaps she and Potter had some other place they shared for their time together.

Lynn went to the kitchenette and started a pot of coffee. He watched her, the quick efficient movements of her hands. She was so damned young, he thought. Could she be much more than twenty, or twenty-one? Perhaps Richard Potter was her first serious love.

"Tell me about Sam Evans," he said, as he watched her measure the coffee into the percolator. "You know him well?"

"It was through Sam that I met Dick Potter," she said. She plugged in the coffee pot and turned toward him. "Sam was a regular at the Greenwich Corner. He—I guess he had a bit of a crush on me. I went out with him a few times, but—well, he's attractive, and charming, and he likes to laugh, but he didn't turn me on the way he hoped he could. One night he brought his boss, Dick Potter, to the Corner and my life was turned upside down in the course of one evening. Sam took it well. Dick is his hero. I was sorry for him, but, God, I was so happy for myself."

"He'd know a lot about Potter's job, wouldn't he?" Peter asked. "More than you do?"

"I don't really know anything at all," she said. "I think Dick was breaking Sam in to do his kind of work for Harkness."

"And he's gone to Carrados—Evans?"

"He was off his rocker from what had happened to Dick, the fact he'd missed the plane, wasn't there at the Carrados airport to help him. He spent the best part of the day before he went down there with me. He asked me questions—questions like you ask. What did I know? Had Dick told me anything that would help?"

"Harkness Chemical sent him down to Carrados?"

"No. He said he'd probably get fired for sticking his nose into the situation, but he was determined to find Dick, or find out why nothing was being done. I think when Wilfred Hadley came back up here and didn't have satisfactory answers for Sam that he went off on his own."

"Would you know how to reach him in Carrados?"

She shook her head. "Only through the company, I suppose."

"If you could reach him could you persuade him to come back here? We need him, Lynn."

"I could try. I suppose if he knew about Hadley—and what you think may have happened—" A little tremor shook her body. "It's hard to believe—that Hadley's death isn't just an accident."

"What about Potter's wife?" Peter asked. "How long have they been married? Would he have talked to her about his work?"

Potter's wife was clearly someone Lynn didn't relish talking about. "They've been married for fourteen years," she said.

"So he's quite a bit older than you."

"If you were interested in me, would you think you were too old?" she asked, almost belligerently.

He smiled at her. "I suppose not."

"I don't imagine Dick's much older than you are," she said.

"Children?" he asked.

"No."

"Something wrong with the marriage or he wouldn't be involved with you. You don't make your relationship with him sound like a simple matter of sexual acrobatics."

She looked away. "I love him and he loves me."

"So why does he stay with his wife?"

"The answer makes it sound as though he was a louse." She was still prepared to fight.

"So tell me why, louse or no louse."

She squared around and faced him. "Dick's wife, Frances, is the daughter of Robert Harkness, the president of Harkness Chemical."

"Oh, for God sake," Peter said. "Why did you wait till now to tell me? That's why Hadley acted so promptly. The boss's son-in-law! And Potter stayed with his wife for the money in it, the job!"

"You don't understand Dick," she said, still fighting. "Harkness Chemical is his whole life. He started there right after he graduated from Harvard—a lawyer. He loves his work. He's fascinated by the whole process of multinational corporate functioning. He'd be lost if he was forced out of it. Would you

33

throw over being a writer and a reporter just for—just for a girl like me?"

"Does Frances Potter know about you?"

"She knows there's someone. I don't know if she knows that it's me."

"And she doesn't kick her husband out on his ear—with papa's help?"

"I—I think she has interests of her own," Lynn said.

"A man?"

"Or men."

"Being a Harkness she might know things about her husband's job, through her father, that you don't know."

"It's possible. They were together a long time before I—before Dick and I—"

"Where does she live?"

"She and Dick have a duplex apartment on Park Avenue." Lynn mentioned an address.

Peter glanced at his watch. "Seven o'clock in the morning isn't an ideal time to go calling on a lady, but maybe I can interest her."

"Won't you wait for the coffee?" she asked, in a small voice.

He was unaccountably angry. People playing cheap games with a man's life at stake, he thought.

"Some other time," he said.

"Please keep in touch."

She was so young, so mixed up.

"I'll see you around," he said.

You didn't just walk up to the door of the Potters' apartment and ring the bell. First there was a doorman, and then a male receptionist in the lobby who looked big enough to be a bouncer in a waterfront saloon. There was no way to get to the elevators without an okay from the person you wanted to visit. That was done through a house phone.

34

An uncultivated woman's voice answered, presumably a maid. Mrs. Potter was not up yet.

"It is an emergency," Peter said.

"You come back later," the maid said.

"Tell Mrs. Potter I have news that relates to her husband," Peter said. "I must talk to her."

"Your name, please."

"Peter Styles."

He waited a long time and then a cool woman's voice came on the line. "I know who you are, Mr. Styles," Frances Potter said. "*Newsview* magazine. You really don't expect me to give you an interview at this time in the morning, do you?"

"I don't want to interview you as a reporter, Mrs. Potter," he said.

"Juliana, my maid, says you have news of Richard."

"I said I had news that related to him. Wilfred Hadley is dead. He was burned to death in the apartment he was using a couple of hours ago. It just may not have been an accident."

"Oh my God!" she said. Then: "You may come up, Mr. Styles."

Peter saw that the receptionist had been listening to the conversation on an extension of the house phone. The man pointed to the elevators.

"Fourteen B," he said.

The maid, probably Puerto Rican, let Peter into the apartment. In the living room, just beyond a vestibule entrance, Peter found Frances Potter. He didn't know what he expected, but certainly not anyone as ravishingly beautiful. She was a complete opposite in coloring to Lynn Mason, raven dark hair, deep violet eyes. She wore a filmy white lace dressing gown that revealed a stunning figure. She didn't look like someone who had been waked out of a deep sleep. Makeup had been subtly applied, every strand of the shining dark hair was neatly in place. Peter had been "looked over" by women before, and he

35

was aware of what was a female appraisal of him as a man, by an experienced woman.

"I apologize for the hour, Mrs. Potter," he said.

"Please, come in," she said. She gestured toward a comfortable-looking arm chair. "Can I have Juliana bring you some coffee?" The voice was low, controlled, used like an actress who understands her instrument. When he shook his head she went on. "How ghastly about Wilfred."

"You knew him?"

"Well. Dick and I spent a summer in Carrados a few years ago. How did it happen?"

"So far they say—smoking in bed."

"But you said it might not be an accident?"

"The autopsy will tell. Actually, the body was so badly burned they aren't sure it is Hadley. They'll have to rely on dental charts. But we do know he was staying in Sam Evans's apartment. There's no reason to think it's anyone else."

She moved, gracefully, to sit on the arm of the couch, only about a yard from him. He was conscious of an unfamiliar but exotic perfume. This was a woman who played the game of being a woman to the hilt.

"How does this relate to Dick?" she asked.

"Hadley was your husband's friend. He tried every way he knew to get your husband released and was fired for his pains."

She frowned. "It was a very complex situation," she said.

"Maybe you can make it simple for me," Peter said.

She hesitated—a stage pause? "If you know that Wilfred was fired you must know why. The Carrados government is threatening to seize Harkness Chemical's assets there. Wilfred had violated their official stand by trying to meet the kidnappers' demands."

"Before the official stand was taken," Peter said.

She smiled at him. "You are up on the details," she said. "An expropriation of Harkness will involve more millions of dollars

36

than you or I can imagine," she said.

"So Harkness makes itself look good by firing Hadley and losing interest in your husband."

"It's not the way it looks, Mr. Styles. Hadley wasn't really fired and he knows it. He's been playing the role of the outraged man but he knew his future was perfectly secure. As for losing interest in Dick, that isn't true, I promise you. But everything has to be done in secret. President Perrault and the Carrados government can't appear to knuckle under to the terrorists. It could result in their overthrow. The United States government doesn't want that. Carrados is a democracy under Perrault. If he were overthrown it would change the whole climate. Harkness doesn't want that. So, publicly, Perrault has taken a strong stand, Harkness is threatened with a severe punishment for bypassing that position. But in secret, both the Carrados government and Harkness are doing everything they can to locate Richard and negotiate for his safety."

"And killed one of the terrorists' negotiators in the process?"

"An unhappy thing, but we still hope—"

"Do you believe in the theory that your husband is somewhere in this country?"

Her smile seemed to tighten and grow fixed. "Lynn Mason supplied that question when we were trying to make sure Richard was alive. No one else had heard of the 'code' she talks about. 'I was concerned about us.' She says that means he's in the United States—'us.' Maybe. Maybe it was just a personal thing between them."

Peter's face had hardened. "I would appreciate it," he said, "if whoever is eavesdropping on our conversation from behind those drapes would come out and join us."

He had seen the movement of the drapes, and then the toe of a man's shoe. Frances Potter stood up, her fists clenched tightly at her sides. She was a very angry woman.

"Come on out, Weldy," she said. "You idiot!"

37

It was a little bit like a stage farce. The draperies were parted and a man, a broad grin on his handsome face, came out. Peter was reminded of a young Clark Gable, good looks, enormous vitality, a kind of amused arrogance.

"Sorry, Frank," he said. "I just stood there a minute to find out if the conversation was private or if anyone could get into it. What a hell of a thing about Wilfred!"

The most arresting thing about this man to Peter at that moment was the fact that he was wearing a white shirt, sleeves rolled up, no jacket, no tie. He looked like a member of the family, his skin tanned to deep bronze color.

"Weldon Keach, Peter Styles," Frances Potter said.

Bells rang for Peter. This was the man who had flown Richard Potter to Carrados on the day of his kidnapping.

"Weldon is an old family friend," Frances Potter said. "He actually flew Richard—"

"I know," Peter said.

Keach's smile was challenging Peter to say anything else he knew.

"I've been frightened to be alone ever since Richard's kidnapping," Frances Potter said. "Weldon's been kind enough to stay here—"

"As a sort of bodyguard," Keach said.

The situation was so transparent Peter would have laughed if he hadn't been angry at their attempt to bluff it out. An ugly thought crossed his mind. Maybe these two obvious lovers wouldn't be too depressed if Richard Potter never reappeared. It made him delay for a moment over his next question.

"I was on my way to talk to Hadley when I walked into the tragedy of the fire," he said. "He knew Carrados so well, the political climate there. Yet he didn't wait at all to try to comply with the terrorists' demands. Didn't he know how the Carrados government would react?"

"He must have thought they'd play along," Keach said.

38

"Release political prisoners?"

"Wilfred must have thought so," Keach said.

Peter turned to Frances Potter, who had relaxed into a sitting position on the arm of the couch again. "That ransom involved not only political prisoners, but millions of dollars in cash. What made your husband so valuable, Mrs. Potter? Hadley didn't wait to consult anyone, he got up the money. He knew, whatever there is to know, about your husband's value to Harkness."

"After all, his wife is Robert Harkness's daughter," Keach said.

"Are you saying that if she had been Minnie McSchmoo from Kalamazoo it would have made Potter less important?"

"Well, wouldn't you?" Keach asked, giving the woman his wide white smile.

"Maybe Potter became important because his wife was a Harkness," Peter said. "Maybe he was moved into an important position for that reason. But the position itself must be what made him so important in Hadley's judgment—and the terrorists' judgment, for that matter. What was his position, Mrs. Potter?"

"Richard didn't talk much about his job."

"Did you have any idea about it?"

She was obviously eager to end this. "The operation of a big multinational corporation like Harkness Chemical isn't something you can learn about over cocktails, Mr. Styles. I don't know why Richard was selected as a victim by the terrorists. I don't know why Wilfred Hadley took it for granted that Harkness would pay anything to get Richard back."

"If you were me, Mrs. Potter, who would you ask, now that Hadley's gone?"

"I could ask my father," she said.

"I'd like to ask him," Peter said.

"Look here, Styles," Keach said, his smile still there but no

39

longer friendly, "Frances has been hanging on by her teeth for months, waiting for some hopeful news about Dick. I think she's had about enough of this third degree."

"I wasn't aware it was a third degree," Peter said. "I hoped you could help, Mrs. Potter. Let me go back to an earlier question. Do you believe your husband may be somewhere here in the United States?"

"If Lynn Mason's trick question is for real—" Frances Potter shrugged.

"I don't believe it for a minute," Keach said. "I flew him to Carrados. They'd keep him there, wouldn't they? He's a bargaining piece. They'd have to be able to produce him if they came to terms."

"This is a small world," Peter said. "A telephone call and Potter walks in the front door here and joins his wife. They don't have to produce him at a specific place."

Keach shook his head. "These terrorists are Latin Americans. They distrust the United States and all its people. They wouldn't believe it was safe to hold a hostage here. Either that wasn't a trick question at all—just a way for Dick to get a personal message to Lynn Mason, or it was a trick question and she has somehow misread the answer. You can bet your last buck that Dick is still in Carrados, or one of the neighboring countries friendly to the terrorists."

Peter looked straight at Frances Potter. "Why would your husband want to send a personal message to Lynn Mason?"

"Because, for Christ sake, they are lovers!" Keach exploded.

Frances Potter's lovely face became unpleasantly hard. "You're going to ask me, Mr. Styles, if I knew that. Yes, I've lived with it for some time. You're going to ask me why I put up with it. Because it left me free to live my own life without questions. Then you're going to ask me if Weldon and I are lovers, and I will answer yes. But if you print it, Mr. Styles, I will sue you and your magazine off the face of the earth."

40

"You left out one question," Peter said. "Why did your husband put up with it?"

"Because he loves his job more than anything else on earth, more than he ever loved me, more than he loves Lynn Mason. A divorce and my father would ship him to the South Pole. It was mutually agreed that we would go our own ways. And now, Mr. Styles—"

The maid, Juliana, came into the room. "A telephone call for the gentleman," she said, indicating Peter.

"May I?" he asked.

Frances Potter indicated an extension on a side table. The caller was Maxvil.

"Lynn Mason said I might find you there," the detective said. "Part of your hunch was right. The dead man in the fire was shot through the heart with a forty-five-calibre slug. No report from ballistics yet—if ever. No gun on the premises."

"I had a feeling," Peter said.

"The rest isn't so good," Maxvil said. "Hadley's dentist says the dead man isn't Hadley. Wrong teeth."

"Oh, brother!" Peter said.

"He could, of course, be a lying sonofabitch," Maxvil said. "They say every man has his price. There's enough money floating around Harkness Chemical to buy thousands of dentists."

3

"Maybe you better go back to Devery's cottage and put your feet up on the table again," Maxvil said.

"Back off, you mean?" Peter asked.

"There was no gun in or anywhere near that apartment," Maxvil said. "You don't shoot yourself in the heart with a forty-five and then have time to dispose of the weapon. This is murder, friend. Someone's prepared to play rough."

Peter and Lynn Mason were in Maxvil's office at police headquarters, a small, uncluttered room. The identity of the man who had been shot and then burned beyond recognition in Sam Evans's apartment was still unknown. Maxvil still toyed with the idea that Hadley's dentist was on somebody's payroll. It seemed important that they get in touch with Sam Evans in Carrados. If the dead man wasn't Hadley, if the dentist was on the level, Evans might be able to tell them who else had access to his apartment. Maxvil had arranged to have Peter bring Lynn Mason downtown to make the call. There was a chance the girl's telephone might not be safe.

"If this phone is tapped, God help us all," he'd said drily.

While they waited for the call to be put through, Maxvil instructed the girl on what to say if they got through to Evans.

"Tell him about the fire and that we believe the dead man is

42

Hadley. No way to tell who's listening in on that end. We haven't given out the dentist's testimony here. The media is just giving out that a man, believed to be Wilfred Hadley, was burned to death in Evans's apartment. Nothing about the dentist or the bullet so far. The word will certainly have gotten to Carrados by now. Let Evans ask questions."

There were two telephone instruments on Maxvil's desk. When a red light blinked on one of them Maxvil gestured to Lynn to answer. As she picked up the receiver on one phone he lifted the other and listened. The operator reported.

"On your person-to-person call to Samuel Evans in Carrados, he isn't there," the operator said.

"When do they expect him?" Lynn asked.

"They don't expect him," the operator said. "There is a Mr. Braden who will take the call if you want to talk to him."

Jesse Braden was the head man for Harkness Chemical in Carrados. They weren't getting office help. Maxvil indicated to Lynn that she should talk to Braden.

"Miss Mason?" A cool, businesslike male voice. "This is Jesse Braden. We've heard the shocking news about Wilfred Hadley. Is that why you're calling Sam?"

"Yes it is, Mr. Braden. I didn't know if the news would have reached you down there. I thought Sam ought to know. I mean, his apartment and all. Can you tell me where I might reach him?"

"He's up there, in New York," Braden said. "He left here yesterday afternoon—commercial flight. He should have arrived in New York some time before midnight last night. He'll surely make contact with the office there when he hears the news."

Maxvil had written something on a piece of paper and slid it across the desk to Lynn.

"Do you know the flight number and the airline, Mr. Braden?"

43

"Avianca, Flight One twenty-six," Braden said promptly. "Due in at Kennedy last night at eleven forty-five." The color of his voice changed. "There's no doubt the man who was burned to death in Sam's apartment was Hadley?"

Maxvil shook his head.

"I don't think there's been an official identification, Mr. Braden," Lynn said into the phone. "But I'm afraid there's not much doubt. I understand Mr. Hadley was living there."

"I'd appreciate if you could keep us posted down here, Miss Mason, if there's any inside scuttlebutt. I know you're concerned about Dick Potter. I'm afraid there isn't anything new. Sam turned the place upside down while he was here, came up with nothing helpful."

"Thank you for coming on, Mr. Braden," Lynn said. "I imagine Sam will be in touch very soon when he's heard the news."

"I'm sure," Braden said. "Perhaps we'll be talking again."

The two phones in Maxvil's office were quietly replaced.

"He came up very quickly with the airline and the flight number," Peter said. "He seems to know all about you, Lynn."

She shrugged. "Office gossip, I suppose."

"And the time of arrival at Kennedy," Maxvil said. He lit his ever-present cigarette. He was frowning. "I don't like the smell of it," he said. He looked at Lynn. "Evans and Hadley were friends? They must have been. You don't lend your apartment to a stranger."

"A stranger who had gone all out for a friend? From what you told me, Lynn, Evans came close to hero-worshipping Dick Potter," Peter said.

The girl nodded. "He loves Dick, tried to model himself after Dick."

"Then Hadley didn't have to be a close friend," Maxvil said.

"I know he'd met him," Lynn said. "He and Dick took several trips to Carrados. I know Sam expressed outrage when

44

he heard Hadley had been fired for meeting the terrorists' demands."

"Frances Potter told me Hadley wasn't really fired," Peter said. "It was a public move to appease President Perrault and the Carrados government. She implied that Hadley knew Harkness would take care of him."

"It would explain something that's been bothering me," Maxvil said. "Look how it went. Potter is kidnapped. A few hours later Harkness Chemical gets the terrorists' demands. Hadley responds instantly—a bonus of a year's salary to three hundred Latin American workers at Harkness. Three hundred workers! I know salaries in Carrados are low, but let's assume five thousand dollars apiece. Would that be high?"

"I'd say right on the nose," Peter said. *"Newsview* said a million and a half at the time."

"And money to feed ten thousand people?"

"Another million and a half," Peter said.

"On the line, just like that, in a matter of hours," Maxvil said. "Hadley couldn't have got his hands on that kind of money without approval from the top. Now they're saying he acted on his own, without authority. They announce they are firing him for that. That has to be part of making things look good for the Carrados government."

"I wonder," Maxvil said. "The whole thing sounds like some kind of cover-up. Suppose—" He let it rest there, staring at the end of his cigarette.

"Suppose what?" Peter asked.

"Suppose Sam Evans got wind of that cover-up in Carrados. He comes high-tailing it back here to confront Hadley with it."

"And finds Hadley burned to death," Peter said.

"So where is he? Why hasn't he surfaced?" Maxvil asked. "And in passing, if that dentist is on the level and the dead man isn't Hadley, where is Hadley? Wouldn't he come forward to let us know he's alive?"

45

"He hasn't heard the news—if he's alive," Peter said. "Not everyone listens to the radio or reads a morning paper. And if he's alive, who is the dead man?"

"I think," Maxvil said, in a flat voice, "I'd like to locate Sam Evans's dentist."

The fire in Greenwich Village and the charred body, tentatively identified as Wilfred Hadley, revived the buried story of the Potter kidnapping on radio, television, and in the afternoon paper. Hadley had negotiated with the Carrados terrorists when Potter had been taken as a hostage over four months ago. People behind the news knew why the story had been buried all this time—or thought they knew. Silence about the kidnapping, they'd been assured, gave Richard Potter his best chance of coming out of the situation alive.

The extra spark that would set the news media on fire had been kept secret by Maxvil and Homicide. The media didn't know about the bullet in the dead man's heart or the negative identification by Hadley's dentist. No hint of murder had reached them yet. But a few relatively independent reporters asked almost forgotten questions. What about Richard Potter? Was there any reason to suppose he was still alive? Was the State Department doing anything on behalf of this American citizen? The CIA was rumored to have helped put the Perrault government into power in Carrados, were they doing anything to help get Potter released? Harkness Chemical said they were doing everything they possibly could to get Potter back, but they had a "no comment" on what that everything was. On an August afternoon in New York not too many people cared much about what had happened to Richard Potter. One man was almost too insignificant to care about. The public had become used to bigger outrages, like the slaughter of the Israeli Olympic team in Munich, like the hijacking of a hundred or more Jewish hostages at Entebbe, like dozens of bombings and

46

senseless massacres of innocent people. One man was almost unnoticeable. Harkness Chemical could afford to pay the ransom. The Carrados government, for past favors, could afford to release political prisoners. Blackmail was nothing new in world politics. People, by and large, were too hardened to horror to be deeply concerned about one man.

Frank Devery was concerned.

The publisher and editor of *Newsview* called a friend on the telephone. The friend was Walter Franklin, a State Department official in New York for a series of conferences with a group of diplomats from what are called "newly emerging nations."

"Do you care, Walter, if we blow this Carrados-Harkness Chemical business sky high in next week's issue?" Devery asked.

"I wish I could say I didn't, Frank."

"Well then, chum, you're going to have to convince me that I shouldn't ask some goddamned embarrassing questions in print. Maybe I can trade you some facts for some facts."

"How do I convince you?"

"You talk to Peter Styles, who is my top man, and you convince him. If he's convinced, then I'll be convinced."

Franklin hesitated. "Styles is a good man," he said. "I've never met him but I know his work. I'll talk to him, Frank, but it's going to have to be off the record."

"This time around, yes," Devery said. "Unless you try to bullshit him. If you do that we'll quote you alongside a full-face picture to run with the story."

Franklin chuckled. "Bullshitting people is my business, Frank. You know that. The gentle art of diplomacy. But I'll make you a promise. I'll tell Styles what I can. There may be some questions I won't answer. But I won't lie to him."

"Fair enough," Devery said.

"And I can't see him till the end of the day. My hotel around seven? I can't cut loose from the United Nations until then."

47

There was most of an afternoon for Peter to wait for his appointment. It was to be an afternoon filled with unpleasant surprises.

Peter hadn't been to his apartment off Irving Place for several weeks. He'd been at Devery's house in the country. He hadn't wanted to go back to the apartment. It was the place where he had lived with Grace. It would be full of memories of her. But they had to be faced sooner or later. He had taken Lynn Mason back to her place and left her there. Her almost-all-night job at the Greenwich Corner made the daytime her sleeping time. He took a taxi across town to Irving Place and let himself into his ground-floor garden apartment.

Surprise number one.

The apartment had been ripped apart, papers, books, clothing from bureau drawers tossed around. Someone had been over every inch of space, down to the jars in the kitchenette that held coffee and sugar and cereal. Looking for what?

He found that the French windows that opened into his small garden had been forced. Someone had come over the back fence to get in. There were things in the place worth stealing that hadn't been touched: several paintings, a silver tea service that had been a wedding present five years ago from the staff at *Newsview,* a small leather jewel box in his handkerchief drawer in the bedroom that contained a set of pearl dress studs and cuff links. It wasn't just an ordinary burglary. Someone had been looking for something specific, and Peter couldn't guess what it had been.

Peter couldn't tell how long ago the search had taken place. It could have been today, it could have been any time in the last three weeks. He had given his cleaning woman a month off while he went to Devery's.

He finally convinced himself it couldn't have anything to do with the Potter case. He'd had nothing to do with it till yesterday, hadn't been involved with the original story when it first appeared months ago. This, he told himself, must have to do with some other story he had been on, perhaps even something to do with Grace, although he'd been here to get clothes before he went to Devery's, after Grace's tragedy had been resolved, finished, written off.

He began the tedious business of trying to restore some kind of order.

The phone rang and it was Maxvil with the second surprise.

"I had a strange feeling about the Mason girl's telephone, which is why I had you bring her down here to make the call to Carrados," Maxvil said. "I sent one of our electronics geniuses up to her building to check out. The lady's phone is bugged."

"Why, for God sake?"

"Somebody may think she knows something. She was Potter's girl. She asked one of the trick questions to determine whether he was alive. They may think he could have told her things they don't want made public. They may know that she was going to you—or someone—to keep the case alive. Maybe they're covering anyone close to Potter."

"Can you trace it?"

"There isn't just someone sitting listening," Maxvil said. "Very sophisticated little tape recorder that's activated the moment she lifts her receiver. We left it there because someone surely must come to collect the tape and put a fresh one into service."

"My place has been ripped apart by someone, top to bottom," Peter said. "I can't believe it has anything to do with Potter, but there it is—"

"I can send someone up there to look for fingerprints," Maxvil said.

"I suppose that makes sense." Peter hesitated. "You left me dangling, Greg, with that remark about looking for Sam Evans's dentist."

49

"If the dead man isn't Hadley, who is he?" Maxvil asked. "I've checked with the airline, Avianca. Flight One twenty-six arrived at ten minutes to midnight last night. Evans was on the passenger list. Why hasn't he surfaced? Where is he? He has to be hiding in a hole somewhere not to have heard the news of the fire and the assumption that Wilfred Hadley was burned to death in his apartment. He hasn't checked with his office. We don't know who his friends are yet, except Lynn Mason. He hasn't called her."

"His dentist?"

"No way to find out who he is without asking him, publicly, to come forward. I'm still letting the assumption that the dead man is Hadley stay up front. Why hasn't *he* come forward?"

"Hadley?"

"Yes. I have an uncomfortable feeling that this may not be a healthy time for Richard Potter's friends. If you stumble on something, Peter—"

"I should get that lucky," Peter said.

"Just bear in mind you're not immortal," Maxvile said. "I'm worried about the girl, too."

"Lynn?"

"She got the ball rolling, didn't she? She got you into the act, and *Newsview,* and me, for God sake! Maybe she should go on a nice long holiday somewhere."

"I think I'd prefer to have her stay around where we can keep an eye on her," Peter said.

Peter spent an hour trying to restore some semblance of order to his place. Then he shaved, showered, and found fresh clothes. At a quarter to six he rang the doorbell at Lynn's apartment.

She let him in, looking bright and chipper. She was wearing a blue-and-red-checked housecoat and she was holding a spatula in her left hand.

50

"You're just in time for breakfast in my cockeyed world," she said.

He went in, accepted coffee and a toasted English muffin while she had eggs and bacon. Whatever her concern for her "guy" there was a wonderful, youthful resiliency here, he thought.

"You know about my phone?" she asked.

"Maxvil told me."

"I would have called you, Peter, but the police said I shouldn't mention it on the phone. In case they want to leave me tapped for a while."

He told her about his apartment, uncertain whether it was connected. "Maxvil's worried about you—and me, for that matter. He thinks there are people who don't want us nosing around. And you might as well know, he thinks the dead man —in the fire—may be Sam Evans. He arrived last night at Kennedy just before midnight. He hasn't shown anywhere, hasn't contacted the office."

"Oh Peter!"

"Who are his friends, do you know? Hadley was living in his apartment. Is there someone he might have asked to put him up?"

Her forehead wrinkled in that little-girl scowl. "It's strange he hasn't called me. He knew how anxious I was to know what he found in Carrados. I don't know about his friends, Peter. I told you, he came to the Corner, I dated him a few times. Single date. Then he turned up with Dick Potter and—and that was that. I hardly saw him again till after Dick was kidnapped. Then he came several times—here. He was very concerned, naturally, and as I told you, he felt guilty. He'd missed the plane."

"You said something about someone slipping him a Mickey."

"He said that. I thought it was just a joking way of saying he'd had too much to drink."

"It was a party? There would have been friends there. Did he say where it was?"

"If he did, I don't remember. It didn't seem important. Then he came and asked me to help with a question for Dick. You know, a question no one else could think up the answer to? So I told him about Dick's and my code. Sam thought that would be fine. We expected Dick to answer it by saying 'I was concerned about Sam.' Sam—South America? But he didn't, and Sam finally wasn't sure it meant anything but just what it seemed to mean. Dick was concerned about us—him and me. I insisted he was telling us he was in the United States. Sam said it wasn't possible." She leaned forward in her chair. "It just can't be Sam, Peter. In the fire, I mean."

"It can be. It can also be someone you and I never heard of. I want you to go somewhere with me."

"Where?"

He told her about his appointment with Walter Franklin, the State Department man. "I'd like you there. You could be helpful."

"How, Peter? I don't see how. I've told you over and over, I don't know anything about Dick's business."

Peter stood up. "I go along with Maxvil," he said. "I don't want you alone."

She laughed. "You planning to spend the rest of your life with me, Peter? It would be nice—but, really, I'm not afraid. Would you believe I have a permit to carry a gun? Late night walk-homes from the Corner with a lot of hopped-up young muggers around."

"Good," Peter said. "Bring it with you."

Walter Franklin was shaggy-haired, a man in his mid-forties, Peter guessed. Everything about him suggested relaxation. His

52

smile may have been professionally cultivated but it was reassuring and warm. He smoked a pipe. He wore a summer tweed jacket with leather patches at the elbows. Peter had called from the house phone in the lobby and announced his arrival. Franklin had suggested his suite would be a nice private place to talk. Peter hadn't mentioned that he had Lynn Mason with him. When Franklin opened the door of his suite only the faintest raising of an eyebrow suggested surprise at seeing the girl. He ushered his visitors in. He had prepared for the occasion. There was a little portable bar, a silver tray of cold eatables.

Peter introduced Lynn as a close friend of Richard Potter's. Franklin was gracious, took drink orders, stayed away from anything more consequential than that it was rather cooler than usual for an August in New York. But finally when they were settled, Peter and Lynn side by side on a couch and Franklin, long legs stretched out, in an arm chair, the State Department man came to the point.

"It's always a pleasure to have an attractive gal present at any kind of conversation. Men usually are at their best in those conditions. But I have to say, Styles, that I told Devery our conversation would have to be off the record. A third person, anyone in addition to you, makes me feel a little hesitant."

Walter Franklin's career was based on dealing with people. He saw in Peter a very tired, very tense man. It was something he hadn't expected. The girl was something else—relaxed, at ease.

"Off the record both ways," Peter said. "I'm going to tell you something the police want buried for the moment. I tell you because you'll know about it through your own sources very quickly. I'd like you not to react to it publicly until the information comes to you that way, not from me."

"Fair enough," Franklin said.

"The man who was apparently burned to death in that Greenwich Village fire this morning was not Wilfred Hadley,"

53

Peter said. "Nor did that man burn to death. He was shot through the heart with a forty-five-calibre slug, the fire set afterwards."

Peter got the impression that Walter Franklin would have taken the news that the hydrogen bomb had been dropped on Detroit with the same lack of emotion that he showed now. He looked at his pipe, saw that it was out, tamped the tobacco down with his forefinger and held his lighter to the bowl.

"The police and I are both concerned for Lynn's safety," Peter said. "I didn't want her left alone until we could arrange for a safe place for her to be. I also thought she might be helpful."

Franklin nodded. The smoke from his pipe curled around his head. "Your news calls for a reassessment of what I assumed were the facts," he said. He looked at Lynn. "I think I must ask you an impertinent question, Miss Mason. All kinds of rumors come to a man in my position. It has been suggested in my hearing that you are something more to Dick Potter than his friend."

"She is," Peter said, eliminating the necessity of a reply from Lynn.

"You are supposed to have provided a trick question for Potter that helped determine that he is still alive—or was at the time he was presented with the questions."

"Yes," Lynn said.

"You have suggested that his answer indicates that he is being held here in the United States."

"Yes."

"Some people think it was just a sort of personal love message from him to you. 'I am concerned about us.' Was that it?"

"Yes." She explained the code; concerned about us meant the United States, concerned about Sam would have meant South America, concerned about you would have meant Europe, concerned about me would have meant the Middle East. "It was

54

just a code between Dick and me," Lynn said. "It was hard not knowing for weeks on end where he was. He couldn't tell me directly, but we worked this out to give me a general idea. There isn't any doubt in my mind that he was telling me that he is being held here, in this country."

"She came to me for help," Peter said.

Franklin gave them an avuncular smile. "I had to be sure that your concern for Dick Potter is primarily personal, Miss Mason," he said, "and that you aren't just a pipeline to higher-ups at Harkness Chemical. Because when I told Frank Devery I'd talk to you off the record, Styles, I didn't mean simply not to be printed, I meant not to be revealed to anyone outside this room. And I have to warn you that the only reason I agreed to talk to you and agree now to talk to Miss Mason, is to try to persuade you to give up looking for Richard Potter and to give up the notion of playing detective in that Greenwich Village murder case."

"Give up!" Lynn said. It was an impulsive protest. The life of the man she loved was hanging by a thread. Give up!

Franklin knocked out his pipe and put it down in an ashtray. Then he took a second pipe from his jacket pocket and began to fill it from an oilskin pouch. "It's a strange thing," he said, in his pleasant, conversational way, "but here you are, Styles, an experienced and gifted reporter, a man of proven courage, who has fought violence of all descriptions including a big corporate power that was responsible for the death of your wife. Yet I suggest you have only a very remote notion of the kind of world you're living in. And you, Miss Mason, involved with a top man in a big power group, and I suggest you, too, have no real concept on the world you live in, the world your Dick Potter lives in. So I'm going to tell you, and God help me, you probably won't believe it. You'll nod, and you'll say 'Yes, of course,' and you won't buy it."

"Try us," Peter said.

55

Franklin lit his second pipe. "We are living in a jungle," he said. "There are no local laws or international laws that can touch it. Every now and then the tip of an iceberg emerges, usually due to some minor malfunction. Take the Lockheed bribery scandal. Two or three political heads were lopped off, but the people shrug and say politics has always been that way, business has always been conducted that way. 'America's business is business' they say, quoting some cynic. These men survive because they are accountable to no one but themselves. They are not accountable to the people, though they talk piously about their stockholders. They are not accountable to their governments, because they have bribed and bought too many politicians to have any fear of any government. They don't believe in a God or have a conscience, so they are not accountable in those terms. So they go ahead in their own sweet way, untouchable except for occasional small fry who get in the way. The people say, 'Surely Harkness Chemical and the democratic government of Carrados won't let Richard Potter die.' I tell you they don't either of them, Harkness Chemical or President Perrault of Carrados, care two cents for Richard Potter. He's a nothing. The people will tell themselves, 'Neither Harkness Chemical nor the democratic government of Carrados would shoot one of their own men in his bed and set fire to his house. That has to be the work of the Mafia or some kind of organized crime syndicate.' I tell you the Mafia, the Syndicate, whatever you want to call them, are kindergarten operators alongside the people I'm talking about. Now, you pry your way into the center of this mess, Styles, and you'll be as dead as last year's political promises. You'll be dead, dead! And if you drag this lovely young lady into it she'll be just as dead as you are." He glanced down at his pipe. "Long speech," he said. He smiled. "Deaf ears, I imagine."

"Not deaf," Peter said. "But not hearing enough. That's the

fight talk before the specifics—I hope." He was aware that Lynn had reached out and that her very cold hand was locked in his.

Walter Franklin looked like a man who wished his visitors had taken his warning and left. Peter thought he was like a tired college professor forced to explain something so elementary that he was mildly irritated.

"There was a time," Franklin said, "when North Americans called the Latin American countries 'banana republics.' If something displeased us down there we sent in a corp of Marines and straightened it out our way. The Marines don't play a big part any more, but you've heard talk that the CIA helped overthrow the Allende government in Chile. The way we do it today. The intellectual leadership of the Third World, the newly emerging nations, on issues of economic development is firmly held by a sophisticated, imaginative, and dedicated group of Latin Americans. They have created the concept of OPEC, the oil-producing countries. They are actively promoting codes of conduct in controlling multinational corporations." Franklin looked unhappily at his pipe which had gone out. "Dry stuff?" he asked. And then without waiting for an answer. "We're not dealing with little tin-star dictators with phoney armies in fancy uniforms. We're confronted by the slickest kind of operators, intellectually shrewder than most of our politicians, ready to seize control of billion-dollar holdings of the big multinationals, supported by communists, terrorists, governments like Cuba's. If they can expropriate Harkness Chemical in Carrados, or Owens-Illinois in Venezuela, or other huge businesses in other places, they will set up a pattern that can be followed by other emerging nations. This isn't a war for territory but a war for markets, and the big multinationals, like Harkness, are trembling in their boots. That, Peter and Lynn, is the geography, the climate into which you're walking to try

57

to save one minnow in a world of sharks. It's too big, too complex, too goddamned powerful for one or two nice people to try to buck."

"And yet—" Peter said. Lynn was gripping his hand as if it was her only chance of survival. The minnow was her man.

Franklin laughed, but there was no humor in it. "It's absurd, isn't it?" he said. "I can reason with the Secretary of State, or the President, or the top corporate leaders in the world, but I can't reason with two children inoculated with some fairy-story kind of heroics. You can't save Dick Potter with your kind of weapons. Hadley is dead or has defected. There isn't a damn thing you can do. If you persist, someone will walk up behind you on the street and stick a hatpin in your heart. A few of us will know why, but not how or who. The killers for these people aren't fanatics, my friends. They are cold-blooded professionals recruited from all over the world. It's a hopelessly uneven battle for you. Two midgets in a world of giants."

"I don't understand," Lynn said, after a moment of silence. "Why do they have to play games? Why don't the terrorists or the Carrados government just seize Harkness Chemical and be done with it?"

"It would take years for them to develop the technical know-how," Franklin said. "And our government, fighting an economic recession, can't let it happen. Would you have guessed that Latin America represents three-quarters of our market for capital goods, nonperishable consumer goods, and chemical products? Money and profits are what matter, Miss Mason, not people. Not Dick Potter." He looked hopeful for a moment and then his face clouded. "So, I've done my best to educate you."

"But nothing to help us," Peter said, his voice harsh.

"I hoped I was helping," Franklin said. He got up from his chair and walked across the room to knock out his pipe in a distant ashtray. "All right. So I will pass on some thinking of mine to you. Potter walks off a company airplane and into the terminal at Carrados and disappears. A few hours later Wilfred Hadley gets the demands; a million and a half in cash bonuses to workers, and a million and a half for food packages to the poor. Just for a moment forget the propaganda and the political prisoners. Does what happen next strike you as odd?"

"What did happen next?" Peter asked.

"Wilfred Hadley produced three million dollars in cash and passed it out."

"So that's what they demanded," Peter said.

Franklin made an impatient gesture. "For God sake, Peter, you don't keep three million dollars in the office safe, or in a shoe box at home! But Hadley had that kind of cash available the minute the demands were made."

Peter's eyes widened. "He knew it was coming? He knew before Potter was kidnapped that it was coming?" Maxvil had suggested something like this.

"How do you read it?" Franklin asked. "The money was ready. He paid it promptly. He 'acted on his own' they said, for which he was later fired."

"If he was fired," Peter said.

"But I don't understand," Lynn said.

"I think Mr. Franklin is suggesting a game we never dreamed of," Peter said. "Harkness Chemical was in on the kidnapping."

"Head of the class," Franklin said. He came back across the room, filling a pipe from the oilskin pouch. "The political situation in Carrados is very touchy. President Perrault represents a group that is essentially democratic, but wobbly. We—the U.S.—support him, which means, I suspect, the CIA supports him. But the terrorists are strong, supported by Carrados's neighbors. So let's say the top brass at Harkness Chemical has come to the conclusion that Perrault's government will fall. They have instantly to find a way to deal with the terrorists who will take over. Under the table they go."

"They make a deal with them?" Lynn asked, wide-eyed.

59

"How much more than three million is involved is your guess," Franklin said. "The terrorists drive a hard bargain. A public payoff that will make them look good. The workers at Harkness get a bonus. The poor get food. The terrorists are heroes to the population. Political prisoners will be freed, and propaganda which they can't circulate gets circulated by Harkness for them. 'You kidnap our man,' Harkness suggests, 'and we will reluctantly—and publicly—pay off. Then, after Perrault's government collapses, we work with you.'"

"Oh God!" Lynn said.

"But something went wrong—a couple of things went wrong," Franklin said. "Hadley, in on the deal, moved a shade too fast for it to look kosher. And Perrault didn't collapse. After two days of anguished decision-making he took a strong stand. No prisoners to be freed and Harkness to be expropriated for going against government policy. For the time being he had moved out of check. So everybody stalls and waits to see what happens."

"For four months!" Lynn said.

"So another pawn gets into the act, your friend Sam Evans. He goes to Carrados to find out what the score is. And what is the score? Has Harkness persuaded the CIA to drop its opposition to the terrorists? Good for business? Because 'business' is our government, God help us. Someone talks to Evans. He gets just a glimmer of the truth, a small piece of it. He suddenly sees Hadley as a villain and hurries back here to face him with it. But someone is a step ahead of him, knows what he is up to. Goodbye Evans. Nobody knows where he is. His remains in that apartment?"

Peter nodded slowly.

"Does what I am saying penetrate at all?" Franklin asked. He sounded almost angry. "State Department policy is to support President Perrault. We approve his stand not to deal with terrorists. It is our stand. But will you believe that I can't tell you where the CIA stands today? Yesterday they supported Perrault. Today they may have shifted sides and are prepared to deal with the terrorists."

"But we are against them!" Lynn protested.

"Who the hell is 'we,' Miss Mason?" Franklin asked. "Harkness Chemical is a huge North American corporation. We do what we can to protect their interests in Latin America and a dozen other places around the globe, just as we protect other huge multinationals. We are against the leftist and the terrorists until it's good for business for us to play ball with them. I may find a directive to that effect when I get back to my desk in Washington."

"That's unbelievable!" Lynn said.

"Why?" Franklin's anger was rising, not against Peter and Lynn but against the situation he was describing. "We fought World War Two against fascism. And when it was over who did we support and do business with? Franco's Spain, the postwar government in Greece, and God knows where else. Fascist governments. It was good for business. Today we piously support Israel. But if the oil-producing countries of the Middle East make the heat hot enough, big business may persuade us to turn our backs on Israel and find pious fault with her. It's a cynical, evil world, Miss Mason." He suddenly struck the back of a chair with the flat of his hand. "I told you this conversation had to be off the record because if what I've said to you were to leak I'd suddenly find myself in a box, investigated by the FBI, my mail intercepted and read by the CIA, my financial life scrutinized by Internal Revenue. So I've risked saying it all to you to convince you that you may not be fighting some wild-eyed radicals and terrorists in Carrados. You may be fighting Harkness Chemical, the CIA, and your own government! You have to quit, and run while the running's good. If if isn't too late!"

"Too late?" Peter asked quietly.

"You've put an honest policeman on the trail, Peter. You've responded to a plea for help from Miss Mason, who's probably been watched since the day Potter was kidnapped. You've come here to me. Were you followed? Have you been aware of surveillance? Of course you'll say no, because you didn't think of it. So it may be too late. But I warn you, if you take one more step in the direction of getting at the truth your chances of seeing the sun rise tomorrow are minimal."

"And Dick Potter is left to die?" Lynn said. Peter could feel her whole body stiffen beside him.

"Yes, he is left to die!" Franklin said. "And Sam Evans, if he's a target. And Wilfred Hadley may be dead. And tomorrow you two may be dead. You are just nuisances in a huge power game. You can't be allowed to rock the boat."

"But what do we do?" Lynn cried out.

"Get Peter to take you to some South Sea island and stay there until this particular war is over," Franklin said.

The hallway outside Franklin's suite at the Beaumont was deserted. The thick carpeting made footsteps soundless as Peter and Lynn Mason headed for the elevators. She was clinging to his arm with both hands. She was fighting tears.

"What do we do?" she asked again, hoping for an answer.

"We take time to put the pieces together and see what we come up with," Peter said.

You sit around parties or in bars or over a lunch table and you talk a nice cynical game about the world in general. It's the smart thing to say that governments have no ethics, that politicians are all bought by lobbyists for special interest groups, that governments act outside the law as revealed by Watergate, that secret motivations and secret plans are always kept from the people, that the people imagine they elect their president and the Congress but the truth is elections are bought by the big power groups. Everything is bought and, in return, paid for. It's wonderful to be cynical like that over drinks, but you go right ahead and vote for the people who are bought.

But there had been nothing cynical about what Walter Franklin had spread out for Peter and Lynn to see. He had been talking facts as he knew them.

The elevator swept them down, still noiseless, to the lobby floor. Here they were suddenly in a crowd of people, some going in to dinner, some headed for the theaters or some night spots. In the background was soft music coming from the Blue Lagoon dining room. Women were dressed for a night on the town, furs in spite of the August weather, jewels. The Beaumont glittered with wealth.

The night bell captain stopped Peter as he and Lynn were headed for the side street exit. The Beaumont was a familiar stamping ground of Peter's and he knew Mike Maggio, the bell captain, with his mischievous gamin face.

" 'Evening, Mr. Styles. Jerry Dodd would like to speak to you for a minute if you can. He's over there by the registration desk."

Jerry Dodd was the hotel's head of security and an old friend.

"Would you mind waiting here for a minute, Lynn?" Peter asked.

She shook her head. She was still in shock, he thought.

Jerry Dodd, a slim, wiry man with very bright black eyes, was an ex-cop and a very smooth operator who helped to keep the Beaumont running like a Swiss watch.

"Hi, Peter," he said. His eyes were never still, watching the people who milled around the lobby.

Peter grinned at him. "You've taken me away from a very pretty lady."

"I didn't see you come in," Dodd said. "Where were you?"

"Visiting a friend upstairs," Peter said. "Walter Franklin, if it matters."

"Someone was looking for you," Dodd said. "No one seemed

63

to know where you were."

"Am I supposed to check in with you, Jerry?"

Dodd frowned. "Something smelled wrong about this guy," he said. "Dark-skinned, little mustache and Van Dyke beard. Spanish, I'd guess, but with a British accent."

"You've got me," Peter said.

"He was insistent about finding you," Dodd said. "I have hunches about people, you know? I didn't think he was a friend. I thought you ought to know."

"Thanks, Jerry, but I haven't a notion who he could be."

"Well, I told you," Dodd said.

"Thanks," Peter said, wondering.

He turned back and headed for the spot where he'd left Lynn.

She wasn't there. He looked around for her. He didn't see her anywhere. He spotted Mike Maggio, the bell captain.

"You see where my lady went to, Mike?" he asked.

"Sorry. Some character got screwed up with his luggage," Mike said. "I wasn't watching."

Peter, a faint feeling of alarm creeping over him, walked over to the revolving door at the side street entrance. She might have stepped out onto the street to get some air, knowing he'd follow her. She wasn't outside.

Peter walked back into the lobby. He headed for Jerry Dodd.

"My girl seems to have walked out on me," he said.

"You losing your touch?" Dodd asked.

Peter gripped Dodd's arm and the security man gave him a surprised look.

"This just could be trouble, Jerry," Peter said.

"The ladies' room," Dodd said, logically.

"Could you make an inquiry for me?" Peter asked. "Miss Lynn Mason."

Dodd headed across the lobby. Peter stood where he was. If he kept moving and Lynn kept moving they might keep missing each other. He didn't see her anywhere. He couldn't imagine

64

why she hadn't stayed put. He didn't want to imagine why she hadn't stayed put.

After a few minutes Dodd came back from the ladies room. "Not there," he said. He recognized anxiety in his friend. "Want me to have some of the boys look?"

"Please," Peter said. "I'll stay put here in case she shows. Long blonde hair, pale blue dress, carrying a leather shoulder bag."

"We'll give it a whirl," Dodd said.

Peter stood waiting, knowing instinctively that it was useless. She wasn't going to show. He felt a cold sweat running down his back inside his shirt.

A few minutes after that Mike Maggio flagged him down.

"Call for you on the house phone, Mr. Styles."

For a moment he allowed himself to feel relief. She was calling him to tell him why she hadn't stayed put. There would be a logical explanation.

He picked up one of the house phones and asked for his call.

The operator's metallic voice said to someone: "I have Mr. Styles for you."

All that happened was the sound of a dial tone. The operator came back on. "I'm sorry, Mr. Styles, but your party seems to have hung up or been cut off."

"I'll wait at this phone, in case they call back."

There was no call back. As he waited, knowing, really, that there wouldn't be a call, he thought he had the message as clearly as if it had been spoken to him. He was to drop his interest in the Potter case or Lynn would pay a price for his stubbornness. What was it Walter Franklin had said? "—inoculated with some fairy-story kind of heroics." That's all he had to use against these people who were so quick, so professional, so final.

PART TWO

1

A combination of physical exhaustion and emotional tensions has a way of paralyzing one's thinking processes. Not crippled by fatigue Peter might have reacted to that penetrating dial tone with some kind of direct action. Instead he hung up the phone like a man in a trance and started to walk across the lobby toward the revolving door at the side exit. Someone checked his progress with a hand on his arm. It was Jerry Dodd, the hotel security man.

"No one seems to have noticed," Dodd said. "Busy time here, people coming and going, no one had any reason to keep an eye on your Miss Mason. You think she just walked off by herself, or would she have been with someone?"

Peter looked at Jerry Dodd, and the security man saw a friend in shock.

"We'll cover the whole bloody hotel," Dodd said. "Where will you be if I come up with something?"

Peter tried to concentrate on Dodd's sharp, anxious face. "I —I don't have any idea, Jerry. Maybe—maybe I'll call you. Thanks for—anything."

Peter started walking toward the exit again. That empty dial tone seemed to ring down the curtain on his ability to function. "A man with a little mustache and Van Dyke beard," Dodd had said. Spanish-looking but with a British accent. He started to turn back toward Jerry Dodd and some sort of automatic braking system stopped him in his tracks. He couldn't lift a finger, he couldn't move in any direction till he knew what had happened to Lynn.

Walter Franklin had been right about the nature of the enemy—too big, too well organized, too powerful for one man to face. He and Lynn had been followed to the Beaumont, and as they were leaving, there had been one moment when the enemy could act. Cold-blooded professionals, Franklin had called them. They hadn't hesitated a second to take advantage of an opportunity.

Why hadn't Lynn cried out, screamed for help? In that crowded lobby she couldn't have been dragged away against her will. Help had been only a few feet away. A gun in her ribs might have convinced her. But so quickly, with no hesitation whatever? If she had argued for ten seconds, Peter would have been back to her.

Peter walked out onto the street. A half moon hung over the city like a lantern at a garden party. He felt like a man handcuffed, bound, and gagged. He was certainly being watched. The enemy would want to know exactly what he did in this new situation. He was a bug under a microscope. A minnow under a microscope, to employ Franklin's image.

Well, what was he going to do? His memory restored the image of Lynn Mason walking up the path to Devery's cottage to ask for help. Every instinct he'd had at the time had told him to turn her off, but he hadn't.

Now she was in double trouble, and there was no move he could make that wouldn't increase her danger.

He had been walking without any direction in mind. A taxi horn blared at him and he found himsself in the middle of Madison Avenue, crossing east against the lights. An early summer evening and there were people out on the sidewalks. He

70

tried to look around him when he reached the safety of the other side of the avenue for a sign of someone following him. It wouldn't be an amateur, he knew. He tried walking fast and then slow, but he couldn't spot anyone behind him or on the other side of the street who was changing pace with him.

Then he realized that he was only a block away from Frank Devery's Beekman Place apartment. The need to share his problem with someone was suddenly overpowering. He walked rapidly now, with a purpose, and he could have sworn that no one had picked up speed behind him. Perhaps they were so sure he would drop it that the microscope was no longer focused on him.

"Jesus, you look terrible!" Devery said when he answered his doorbell and saw Peter.

There was a mirror in the vestibule and Peter caught a glimpse of himself in it. His eyes were sunk in dark hollows, his face twisted out of shape.

Devery poured a stiff drink without asking. The French windows to his terrace overlooking the East River were open. He'd evidently been sitting out there. Peter sank down in a comfortable wicker arm chair on the terrace, convinced he would never get out of it again.

He told his story to Devery in bits and pieces, stopping to gulp at his drink and to catch his breath, like a tired runner.

"So I am out of it," he said, finally. "No choice. And God knows who can do anything for anybody."

Devery hadn't commented. He asked: "Were you followed here?"

"I don't know," Peter said, wearily. "I couldn't spot anyone, but I don't know."

"They're not magicians!"

"Who says so?" Peter realized he wanted to laugh and that it was close to hysteria.

"We better get in touch with Maxvil," Devery said. "He

knows the city. He may be able to get us some kind of lead to the girl."

"Get on her trail and she's probably dead!" Peter said. "We're trussed up like a Christmas turkey, Frank."

"I'll call Maxvil," Devery said, and went back into the apartment.

Peter sat motionless, looking down at the twinkling lights of a barge that floated slowly down the river toward the sea. He didn't want to move. He didn't want to do anything, face anything. He wanted to forget the last months of his life. He wanted peace somewhere, and quiet, and the ability to black out the past. He had tried to help a girl who was in his kind of trouble and he simply didn't have the equipment to deal with her problem.

The barge slipped slowly out of his line of vision and he closed his eyes. They felt hot and dry.

Devery came back onto the terrace. "Maxvil is stuck for the moment," he said. "It'll be an hour or more before he can get up here. Come into the bedroom and lie down."

"I don't want to move, Frank."

"Move! Take your clothes off, take a hot shower, lie down. An hour's sleep is better than no sleep. When did you sleep last?"

"Last month, last year," Peter said, and that crazy desire to laugh welled up again.

The steaming hot shower was unbelievable medicine. Devery had laid out a robe for him and he just managed to get it on before his head touched the pillow and he was out cold.

Unreasonable, unfriendly hands shook him. He opened his aching eyes and saw Maxvil.

"Sorry to have taken so long," Maxvil said.

"Long! It was only a moment ago that—"

"Two hours," Maxvil said. "The CIA has been on my back telling me how to handle the fire murder. You want a drink?

72

Coffee? Just lie there and tell it to me horizontally."

Devery was standing in the doorway. He held a legal pad and a ballpoint pen. He was going to take notes this time.

It was less painful to tell the second time around. When he had finished Maxvil asked for a detailed account of what Walter Franklin had said about the situation. The detective listened, nodding from time to time.

"What was it I said?" he asked when Peter had finished. "Five roads to death. You can be up against any one of five groups who want you dead—or a combination of several of them."

"I'm out of it," Peter said. "Lift a finger and Lynn Mason has had it."

"Who says so?" Maxvil asked. He was tilted back in a chair beside the bed, his eyes squinted against the smoke from his cigarette.

"Nobody had to say it," Peter said. "It's what you cops call their M.O., isn't it? Method of operation? These people use kidnapping to get something they want. They want me to drop my investigation of the Potter case."

"Why?" Maxvil asked. The corner of his mouth twitched in a bitter little smile. "What have you done that's so dangerous to them? Given a little girl hope by promising her help you aren't able to give? That doesn't make you very dangerous to them."

Peter raised himself up on his elbows. "Cut it out, Greg! I'm not in the mood for wisecracks."

"I'm dead serious," Maxvil said. "What makes you dangerous? You're a good investigative reporter. So are a lot of other people. So to silence you they stage the riskiest abduction I ever heard of! They snatch a girl, right in the middle of a crowded hotel lobby, where one squeak for help would have had dozens of people rushing to her. They could have picked her up five minutes later on the street without much risk, or later tonight

73

in her apartment without much risk. But no, they snatch her in the most public place I can imagine, with help at her elbow and professional help in the person of Jerry Dodd only a few yards away. You call them cold-blooded professionals. I call them crazy."

"So, crazy or not, they made it," Peter said.

"I think I doubt it very much, Peter," Maxvil said. "I think the lady walked out on you. Nobody would have stopped her, or noticed anything unusual, if she just walked away."

"No!" Peter said. He swung his legs over the side of the bed and sat up straight. "We'd talked about the possible danger we were in. She simply wouldn't walk away without telling me where she was going."

"Think of any conditions under which she might?"

"No."

"I can think of two," Maxvil said. He took a deep drag on his cigarette. "How does the song go? 'Some enchanted evening —across a crowded room'? Suppose, Peter, she looked across that crowded lobby and saw Richard Potter. Would she have stopped to tell you?"

"That's crazy!"

"Maybe. What if she saw Sam Evans—whom we've all just about decided to mourn as dead? Does she run to you and say 'I think I just saw Sam Evans across a crowded room'? Like hell. She hurries over to get her hooks into him before he disappears. No time to hold a conference with you."

"Same thing would hold if she saw Wilfred Hadley," Devery said from the doorway. "If she knows him by sight."

It made sense. It made just a little sense.

"Who called me on the house phone?" Peter asked.

"Maybe she did," Maxvil said. "Thought she had a minute to explain and—" he shrugged—"the minute evaporated. Maybe she's trying to call you now, only she has no idea where you are."

As if on cue the bedside telephone rang. Devery crossed and picked it up. It was evidently someone he knew—but not Lynn. For just a moment Peter had hoped.

"Yes, he's here," Devery was saying. He held the phone out to Peter. "Your friend Jerry Dodd at the Beaumont."

"Sorry, Peter, nothing on your lady friend," Dodd said when Peter answered. "Thin air department on her. But the fellow I told you was asking for you—the Spanish-looking guy with the British accent?"

"What about him?"

"He fell, or was pushed, or was slugged and then pushed, down the back fire stairs from the lobby to the first-level basement. They've carted him off to Bellevue Hospital. Emergency doctor didn't give him much chance."

"Identification?" Peter asked.

"Nothing on him, except a shoulder holster with a thirty-eight police special in it."

"You think he is a cop?" Peter asked.

"Who knows?" Dodd said. "Could be undercover, I suppose. Labels cut out of his clothes. No wallet. No driver's license or credit cards. I thought you ought to know. I didn't know where to reach you so I tried your boss when your own phone didn't answer. This character was real interested in you, Peter."

"I hope he doesn't take off before we can talk to him," Peter said.

"Don't worry, pal," Dodd said. "This guy isn't going to take off for anywhere for a while—unless there really is a heaven or a hell."

It wasn't a new experience for Peter. He had set out on dozens of stories in his time with little or nothing to go on. In the early stages some kind of defeatist impulse urged him to abandon the hunt for information, look for something else. More than once he had found his personal emotions involved

75

so that his skills as an investigator were blunted.

Two days ago he had been sitting on the terrace of Devery's cottage indulging himself with the pain of his own tragedy. He had stopped being who he really was. Lynn Mason had persuaded him to get back into action again, and he had moved, uncertainly. A little more than two hours ago she had disappeared, and he had slumped back into a state of helplessness. It was as if he had chosen, secretly, not to try to help any more, not to be himself. Why not? He had lost the drive that had made him one of the top men in his profession.

Now, as he dressed hurriedly in Devery's bedroom, he felt somehow revived, renewed. It wasn't the first time in his career that Greg Maxvil had turned him around and forced him to face a problem from a new perspective. Maxvil had a genius for looking at a case from half a dozen different points of view.

The detective was right, of course. Lynn Mason would never have allowed herself to be marched out of that crowded lobby without any kind of protest. She was a gutsy girl. She must have moved away from the spot where Peter had left her of her own volition. It couldn't have been that she saw Richard Potter. He was in enemy hands. It could have been Sam Evans. It could have been someone she hadn't mentioned whom she thought could help. What had happened then? She couldn't have meant to leave Peter high and dry.

It was something to work on, a live trail. And the Spanish-looking man with the British accent was a live trail. At least they knew where to locate him. Peter remembered his college football days, coming out of the locker room after a bad first half, ready to play to win. That was how he suddenly felt now.

The man who had fallen down the stairs at the Beaumont, the man who had been so insistently curious about Peter, was in the intensive care unit at the hospital. Maxvil's badge got them past the normal barriers to the doctor who was handling the case.

76

"Badly fractured skull," the doctor told them, "a broken arm and some broken ribs. The head wound is the one that matters. The odds are pretty heavily against his making it, Lieutenant."

"He can't talk?"

"Lord, no. Not now, maybe never."

"Could all the injuries have come from an accidental fall?" Maxvil asked.

"Could," the doctor said. "Stone steps, an iron handrail on both sides."

Something in the doctor's voice made Peter ask: "But you don't think so, Doctor?"

"The skull damage appears to have resulted from four or five severe blows landing in almost exactly the same place. Picture a man somersaulting down a flight of stairs. How likely is it that he would hit his head in exactly the same place, inflicting exactly the same kind of injury, half a dozen times?"

"You think he was slugged?" Maxvil asked.

"My guess," the doctor said.

"We were told he had nothing on him in the way of identification," Maxvil said.

"Depends on what you mean," the doctor said. "No wallet, no cards or licenses, no letters. Even the labels were cut out of his clothes. He was carrying a gun which I suppose you people might trace. But there are always ways of identifying a man if you have the right people to ask."

"Dental charts, you mean?"

"If you can locate his dentist," the doctor said. "This man has an appendix scar, operation some years ago I'd say. He's missing the little toe on his left foot. Of course there are finger-prints. A policeman on duty here has already taken them. I suppose your department, or the FBI, might be able to match them up with some kind of record."

"I have a special interest in those prints," Maxvil said. He glanced at Peter. "This guy was so interested in you he just

77

might be the one who took your apartment apart." He turned to the doctor. "Any chance of having a look at him?"

"Nothing to see but bandages," the doctor said.

The next stop was the Beaumont and Jerry Dodd. The hotel's gracious lobby was quiet now, people drifting in sporadically from the theater or some other socializing. Soft music came from the Blue Lagoon Room where people still danced to old-fashioned rhythms.

Maxvil wanted a clear picture of how things had been when Lynn disappeared. Peter showed him where he'd left her, where Dodd had been standing near the reservation desk.

"You have to visualize a lot of people in between us," Peter said. "The lobby was crowded."

"Theater-going time," Dodd said. "People coming out of the bars and the dining rooms. Everyone seems to leave at once."

"How long was your conversation?" Maxvil asked.

"Thirty seconds," Dodd said, and Peter nodded.

"So she had to have taken off the minute you left her," Maxvil said.

"Working my way across the lobby, talking to Jerry, going back—no more than a minute and a half," Peter said.

"A fast mover, your Miss Mason," Maxvil said. He asked to see the place where the man in the hospital had taken his fall.

In a building like the Beaumont the fire stairs are inside, running from floor to floor, carefully insulated, windowless. This one was clearly marked FIRE EXIT in a horizontal red light.

"You have four exits to the street on this level," Maxvil said. "Why a fire exit?"

Dodd shrugged. "Leave nothing to chance. Main doors could be blocked. But, of course, it's a way up from the basement levels."

"No way out to the streets from down there?"

"Sure. But they could be blocked."

They opened the fire exit door and stepped into a concrete-

78

lined area way, a fairly broad landing. A concrete stairway came down from the floor above, another led down to the basement.

"They found your friend down at the bottom—one of the maintenance men," Dodd said.

"But nobody saw him fall?"

"No. He was out cold, lying in his own blood."

"What about up here? Signs of a fight or a struggle of any kind?"

"Nothing here on the landing," Dodd said. "But blood spots all the way down the stairs. The police took pictures."

"No weapon? The doctor thinks he was slugged."

"Nothing. Cops looked all over."

"Anybody see our man—or anyone else—come out here through the fire exit door?"

Dodd shrugged. "The place was jammed. Who notices? Oh, I would have if I'd been looking this way. Asked myself why. Some of the staff might have asked why if they'd seen. But apparently nobody did."

"Let's suppose he followed somebody out here," Maxvil said. "That somebody has spotted him, knows he'll be following, waits, and pistol whips him when he arrives. I suggest he was beaten with a gun butt because a gun would be easy to carry away. Our man falls down the stairs. The attacker could just walk out into the lobby into the crowd."

"He could have gone down to the lower level to see what shape the other guy was in," Dodd said. "Find his way to the street from down there."

"Nobody down below saw him?"

"No."

"And nobody up at this level in the lobby?"

"I keep telling you—"

"I know. The lobby was crowded. No one had any reason to pay attention." Maxvil leaned against the stair rail and lit a

79

cigarette. "The guy in the hospital is bandages from head to foot. A mummy, for God sake. You think you could work with a police artist to give us a likeness of him?"

"Why not," Dodd said.

"Tell me about him," Maxvil said.

"I didn't notice him come in," Dodd said, "but I had seen him circulating around the lobby, looking for someone, I thought. Neatly trimmed beard and mustache. Short hair, not a hippie type. Good suit—but foreign tailored, tight fitting, narrow pants. Things I notice. Dark skin. I figured him for some U.N. character, maybe an Arab or Lebanese. We have a lot of them around here. Then suddenly he headed straight for me where I was standing, as though he knew who I was. Maybe I look like the help. Do I know Peter Styles, he asks me. I tell him yes. Have I seen Peter around? No, I tell him. British accent he has. Not unusual, you understand. A lot of these Middle Eastern guys are educated in England. Then I got the notion he was Spanish. When I said I hadn't seen you, Peter, he muttered something under his breath. It was Spanish or Portuguese. I don't speak either, you understand.

" 'I saw him come into the hotel just a few minutes ago, from across the street,' he said to me. 'With a lady.' "

"Well I hadn't seen you, so I told him I was sorry. I suggested he have you paged. You could be anywhere with a lady—the Trapeze Bar, the Blue Lagoon, the Concord Room. He said he'd just look. I don't know why, but I had an uneasy feeling about him. I thought he wasn't a friend of yours, Peter."

"And that was all?" Maxvil asked.

"I saw him head for the Trapeze Bar on the mezzanine. That's the last I saw of him. About an hour later I spotted you, Peter, with the lady coming out of the west elevators. I sent Mike Maggio to flag you down. I thought maybe you better know this guy was looking for you."

So much for that until a little later in the evening. The police had been to Peter's apartment and lifted several promising prints. Shortly before midnight Maxvil called.

"Our friend in the hospital was your burglar," he said. "You figured out yet what he could have been looking for?"

Peter hadn't the remotest idea. He had gone back to his apartment after the session with Dodd at the Beaumont. If Lynn was operating on her own she surely would try to reach him. He'd spent more than an hour trying to restore order to his place and he couldn't find a single thing missing.

Nothing from Lynn. About one o'clock he called the Greenwich Corner and asked for her. They were concerned there. She hadn't shown up for work.

2

Maxvil's theory about Lynn's disappearance had been reassuring at first, but as the night wore on without any word from her the picture grew darker again. Waiting was almost unendurable. Somebody else was holding all the cards and playing them. Walter Franklin's warning about the power of the forces involved was hard to shake, and it produced a feeling of helplessness. The need to move was immense, and yet Peter had no notion where to start.

At two o'clock his phone rang, and he sprang for it.

"Mr. Styles?" A strange male voice, young sounding.

"Yes."

"You don't know me, Mr. Styles. My name is David Willis. I know this is a terrible time to call, but I don't have any choice."

"What can I do for you?" Peter asked.

"A friend of mine is in some kind of trouble," the young voice said. "He told me if it came to that I was to call you."

"Who is your friend?" Peter asked.

"His name is Sam Evans," the voice said.

Peter felt his hand tighten on the receiver. "I don't know anyone named Sam Evans," he said, which was the literal truth.

"You may have heard of him," Willis said. "He was associated with a man named Richard Potter who was kidnapped in South America about four months ago. Your magazine covered the story."

"I think I remember," Peter said. "What kind of trouble is Evans in?"

"It's too complicated for me to try to tell you on the phone," Willis said. "I wonder if I can come to see you? I know it's an outrageous time of night, but, frankly, the hell is scared out of me, Mr. Styles."

"I don't understand why you're calling me," Peter said.

"Because Sam told me to."

"Evans told you to call me?"

"Yes."

"But I've told you I don't know him."

Willis sounded desperate. "I know that, Mr. Styles. But Sam said you were the only person he could think of who might help him out of his trouble."

"Evans said that?"

"You have a reputation, Mr. Styles, as an investigative reporter. I think Sam thought it would be like calling Carl Bernstein or Bob Woodward of the Washington *Post*—if you were in Washington. He told me if I didn't hear from him in any twenty-four-hour stretch I should go to you for help. It's twenty-six hours since I've heard from him."

"Why did you wait?"

"Because I kept hoping. Now I don't have any choice. Something bad must have happened to Sam."

"I can't leave here," Peter said. "Where are you?"

"Fortieth Street and Park Avenue."

"A taxi should get you here in ten minutes," Peter said, and gave Willis the address.

"I'm terribly grateful to you, Mr. Styles."

One of the things the Spanish-British burglar had left untouched was Peter's gun. He kept it, very casually, in his handkerchief drawer along with the leather jewel box in which he kept his dress studs. The handkerchiefs had been taken out of the drawer and scattered on the bureau top, the jewel box opened and left that way, but with nothing taken. The gun, for which Peter had a permit, had been moved around but had been of no interest to the searcher. Peter slipped the little flat handpiece into his jacket pocket and went back to his living room to wait for Mr. David Willis.

There was something screwy about Mr. Willis and his call. A total stranger in trouble doesn't call on a total stranger for help. And yet it had happened once before in the last thirty-six hours. Lynn Mason had come to Peter for help, Peter, a complete stranger, but a man who had for a long time conducted a public crusade against violence. In that sense he wasn't a stranger to her or perhaps to Sam Evans.

As he waited it occurred to Peter that there was a chance Willis was actually coming with some kind of message from Lynn. She might not want to talk on the phone. She had reasons to distrust phones. The mention of Sam Evans would make Peter hold still until Willis could get the real message to him. He hoped it might be that way.

It took David Willis twelve minutes to get to Peter's doorbell. His appearance went with the young-sounding voice. He was tall, slim, owlish-looking behind shell-rimmed glasses. His reddish brown hair was worn rather long, and he had on what Peter guessed was a Brooks Brothers' tropical worsted summer suit in pale grey. He looked about twenty-five years old at most. His smile was apologetic.

"It's terribly good of you to let me come, Mr. Styles," Willis said, hesitating outside the open door.

"Come in," Peter said. "What you told me doesn't make much sense, but I couldn't resist hearing more."

Willis came in, sat down on the edge of the chair that Peter indicated. He was obviously eager to get to his point, whatever it was.

"Sam felt that you were the one person on the other side who might understand his situation without long explanations. Explanations I'm not equipped to give you, Mr. Styles."

"What do you mean 'on the other side'?" Peter asked.

"I think—I think he really meant on the outside," Willis said. "It's all connected with the Potter kidnapping. On the inside are the kidnappers, the government of Carrados, Harkness Chemical, our government. You, as a reporter, are on the outside. But interested. Sam thought you would have to be interested."

Peter smiled. "You're doing a good job of interesting me, David. So just get to it."

Willis moistened his lips. "I don't quite know where to begin because I don't know how much you know."

"I know what *Newsview*'s staff dug up at the time," Peter said. "Evans was Potter's assistant. He was supposed to make that fatal trip to Carrados with Potter but he missed the plane. That's what I know about your friend Evans." Let it come from Willis, Peter thought.

"He thinks he was drugged, you know," Willis said.

"Drugged?"

"So that he would miss the plane. That was four months ago."

Peter didn't add "and fourteen days."

"In the very beginning it looked as though the kidnappers' demands would be met, and then the Carrados government backed off."

"That I know."

"A man named Wilfred Hadley, who was handling the negotiations, was fired by Harkness and came back to this country. Sam went to him to find out what the score was. Sam

85

was pretty upset by what Hadley told him."

"What did Hadley tell him?"

"I don't know. Except that there was double dealing on all sides. Sam decided to go to Carrados to try to find out for himself. He loaned Hadley his apartment in the Village."

"Where Hadley was apparently burned to death last night."

"You know that?"

"My dear David, it's been on the radio, on television, and in the papers. Everybody knows that. Could we get to the reason for your coming here?"

Willis got up from his chair and began to move, restlessly, up and down in front of Peter. "Sam got back from Carrados last night," he said. "He called me from Kennedy shortly before midnight. He sounded excited—very uptight, if you know what I mean. 'I may be walking right into a trap,' he told me."

"Did he say what kind of a trap?"

"He sounded in a hurry, but he wanted help," Willis said. " 'I need you to be my life insurance,' he said. 'I think I've found out that the top brass in Harkness are playing along with the terrorists. Maybe they planned the whole thing together.' It sounded wild to me, but he didn't try to explain."

Not so crazy that Walter Franklin hadn't already suggested it, Peter thought.

"There's just one man who can help Dick, unless he's in on it himself,' Sam said. Then he said: 'The girl was right. Dick's somewhere in this country.' "

"What girl?" Peter asked, his face expressionless.

"Potter has a girl," Willis said. "Her name is Lynn Mason. She had some sort of code thing with Potter. They used it to ask questions to make sure he was alive. The girl insisted that Potter's answer meant that he was somewhere in the United States. Nobody believed it. Sam didn't believe it, although he thought the girl wasn't playing games. When he called me last night he had changed his mind. 'The girl was right,' he said."

86

Peter tried a smile. "We were headed for a trap, David," he said. Willis had paused near the sideboard-bar in the corner of the room. "Help yourself," Peter said.

"I'd be most terribly grateful," Willis said. He poured a straight slug, and the neck of the bottle stuttered against the rim of the glass. He swallowed the drink in one gulp and turned back to Peter. "The trap," he said.

"That's where you were headed."

"There is a man here in New York named Gabriel Zorn," Willis said. "He's head of security for Harkness Chemical, as I understand it. Dick Potter and Sam work very closely with him. It's part of their job—undercover stuff, you know. Sam thought of Zorn as an experienced, wise friend. Zorn would be the most natural person for him to go to for help, after Potter, if he was in a jam. That's where he was going last night when he called me."

"To see Zorn?"

"Yes. He was going straight from the airport."

"The trap, David. You've got my tongue handing out. Sam Evans was going to see his friend Zorn. Where is the trap?"

"That's it," Willis said.

"Come again."

"That was what Sam thought might be the trap," Willis said. " 'Gabe Zorn is the only person I can go to with what I found out in Carrados,' he said. 'But if it should turn out that Gabe is in on it with the rest of them I've had it.' That's what he said, Mr. Styles. He wasn't sure about the only man he might be able to trust. That's where you came into it."

"I don't get it. If he didn't trust Zorn, why go to him?"

" 'If I can't trust Gabe, the ball game is over,' is what he said. 'If I don't call you back within twenty-four hours, you've got to help me, David,' he said. Of course I said I would."

"And your help was to consist of calling me?"

"Yes. If he didn't call me, it would mean he was in big

trouble. If Zorn turned out to be involved, turned out to be the enemy, then there was no point in going to anyone on the inside —in the Harkness setup—for help. No one could be trusted if Zorn couldn't. And no one in the State Department, he said, or the CIA. The only help could come from the outside, someone not possibly involved who would understand 'the way the game is played,' he said. 'Peter Styles can be trusted. He's been involved in this kind of thing himself. Try to persuade him.' So—" Willis spread his hands.

"And what am I supposed to do?"

"God knows, Mr. Styles. I haven't the faintest idea. Sam seemed to think you would know."

"Sam is a dreamer," Peter said. He stood up, his muscles feeling cramped from long sitting. He crossed over to the bar and fixed himself a drink. Willis stood there, staring at him like a hopeful spaniel puppy. A strange messenger to send, this boy. "He never called you back?"

"No, and I stayed by my phone the whole time—until I called you. I waited beyond the twenty-four hours because I kept hoping—any minute—"

"He went to see Zorn?"

"That's where he said he was going."

"But he never called back to say he had?"

"No."

"Did he mention Wilfred Hadley in his conversation with you?"

"No."

"Did he say anything about going to his apartment before he went to see Zorn?"

"No. I've told you exactly what he said."

"Had he ever asked you for help like this before?"

"No."

"Why do you suppose he chose you? And why do you suppose he didn't call me himself if he thought I could help?"

"He said he'd tried. He said you didn't answer your phone. I—I think he chose me to call you because I was the only close friend he had who wasn't somehow involved with his job, his work. We went to school and college together. I—I was a couple of years behind him, but we'd been close for a long time. I was a logical choice, I think."

"He could have waited until he could reach me himself," Peter said. If Evans had called Willis from the airport that must have been just before midnight. The Avianca flight had arrived at 11:50. At that time Peter had been at the Greenwich Corner listening to Lynn Mason perform.

"I think he couldn't wait," Willis said. "I think he was afraid if he delayed, it might put Dick Potter in danger."

Peter went over to the telephone table and thumbed through the Manhattan directory. There was no telephone listed in the name of Gabriel Zorn. He tried information. No phone in Zorn's name, not even unlisted according to the operator. Maxvil could have pried an unlisted number loose if there was one.

"What are you going to do?" Willis asked.

"Locate Gabriel Zorn," Peter said.

Devery, muttering about Peter's never sleeping, confirmed the existence of Zorn when Peter phoned.

"I don't know anything about him," Devery said, "but he was a part of the story at the time Potter was kidnapped. Chief of security for Harkness Chemical. He isn't an undercover operator, phone or no phone."

Maxvil was more helpful. "Former agent for the CIA," he said when he'd heard Peter's story. "Moved over to Harkness about five years ago. Give me fifteen minutes and I'll locate him for you."

"I wondered if Frances Potter might have a number for him," Peter said. "I'm told Richard Potter and Evans worked

89

closely with Zorn. She might know."

"You don't want to wait till he shows up at his office in the morning?"

"I quote you," Peter said. " 'Time is the enemy.' "

"Let me call Mrs. Potter," Maxvil said. "I have a feeling she doesn't love you after your visit yesterday morning."

Peter started the coffee percolator going and it was just ready to pour when Maxvil called back.

"The lady was most cooperative," he said. "She gave me a number for Zorn. Seems he's been keeping an eye on her since the kidnapping. Company policy! The telephone people have given me an address for the number. I'll pick you up in fifteen minutes."

"You're going to see him?"

"More official and effective than a reporter from *Newsview*," Maxvil said. "I'm investigating a homicide, remember? The victim may be Hadley, may be Sam Evans. Logical for me to wake up the Harkness security chief at four in the morning. Not so logical for you. But you'll be with me. You heard from Evans.— And Peter?"

"Yes."

"Your young friend there is to keep his mouth shut. Talk to no one, understand? He never heard from Evans. Tell him he may get in big trouble himself if he spills to the wrong people. Maybe he'd better just stay there in your place till we've heard Zorn's story."

The name Gabriel Zorn suggested some kind of character. The chief of security for Harkness Chemical didn't disappoint them. He lived in a ground-floor apartment in a remodeled brownstone in the East Sixties. Maxvil and Peter hadn't called Zorn to announce their coming, they just arrived and rang his doorbell. The ring was answered promptly enough by a harsh-sounding voice, asking who it was.

"Police," Maxvil said. "Lieutenant Maxvil, Homicide."

There was a short delay, and then the door was opened by a man who looked to be right out of a television melodrama. He was big, paunchy, with close-cropped grey hair. His heavy jowled face was rock hard, grey eyes narrowed. He held a cannon-sized handgun aimed directly at Peter and Maxvil.

"Identification," he said.

Maxvil produced.

"And who is this one?" Zorn asked, nodding at Peter.

"Peter Styles, a writer for *Newsview* magazine," Maxvil said.

"You carry your own press man around with you, Lieutenant?"

"When he has information," Maxvil said.

Zorn seemed to relax, slightly. "I suppose you can come in," he said. He was wearing a seersucker robe over dark blue pajama bottoms. He was barefooted. A nest of bristly grey hair showed on his chest. "Hell of a time to make a call, Lieutenant," he said.

The room they entered was monastically plain. The walls were painted a dull grey, no pictures or decorations of any sort. A plain kitchen-type table and four kitchen chairs. It didn't look lived in. Beyond this room must be a bedroom, a bath, perhaps a small kitchen. But doors to other rooms were closed.

"I suppose you're here about my man Hadley who was burned up in a fire yesterday," Zorn said. He breathed hard, like a man with some kind of chronic bronchial difficulty. He didn't suggest sitting down, but he did slip his handgun into the pocket of his robe. His hands were huge, their backs hairy. He must, Peter thought, have been a powerful giant a few years back. The remnants of that powerhouse must be about sixty years old now.

"The fire was the starting point," Maxvil said. "I suspect you've had your ear to the ground, Mr. Zorn."

"Meaning what?"

91

"That you know the dead man was murdered, not burned to death. That you also know that Wilfred Hadley's dentist says the dead man isn't Hadley."

"You haven't made that public," Zorn said.

"But no use pretending with you, is there, Mr. Zorn?" Maxvil said, smiling cheerfully.

The heavy jowls quivered slightly. "So what can I do for you?"

"Help me to identify the dead man would be a start," Maxvil said. "Tell me where Hadley is would be another start."

Zorn reached into the pocket of his robe and produced a crumpled package of cigarettes. He went into a paroxysm of coughing as he inhaled the first bit of smoke.

"Those things aren't good for you," Maxvil said. "Should we start with Hadley and where he is?"

Zorn got control of his cough. "I don't know where he is," he said. "I've been trying to locate him ever since I heard the dead man was someone else."

"Who did you hear that from, Mr. Zorn?" Maxvil asked, still cheerful.

"We were concerned at Harkness," Zorn said. "Hadley is our man. Ears to the ground."

"I suggest the dentist," Maxvil said. "He's a company man too, isn't he?"

"You must have found that out when you checked on him," Zorn said.

Maxvil nodded. "Thinking he might have been bought," he said.

Zorn covered any reaction to that comment by another mild coughing spell. "Of course he wasn't," he said. "Bought by who?"

"Just about to ask you that," Maxvil said. "But Hadley isn't really why we're here, not primarily. We think the dead man may be Sam Evans, another of your boys."

92

Zorn looked genuinely surprised. "It's his apartment, I know, but Sam is in South America."

"Not so, Mr. Zorn." Now Maxvil wasn't smiling. "Sam Evans landed at Kennedy Airport night before last at ten minutes to midnight. He made at least two telephone calls from the airport. One call involved a message to Mr. Styles, here, and the other, we're told, was to you."

"You were told wrong," Zorn said. "Sam never phoned me. I tell you, until this minute I thought he was in Carrados."

"I don't believe that."

"Well, screw what you believe, Lieutenant. I'm telling you how it is."

"I can just imagine your office at Harkness," Maxvil said. "Diagrams and charts, and names printed on little tabs that you can slide into different holders. Mr. A has gone from New York to Carrados, you move his name tab from one board to another. Mr. B is in Paris, you slide his name into the Paris board. Something like that, isn't it? You know, every minute of every day and night, just where anyone of any consequence is. His name is in the right place on the boards. So how come you haven't known for approximately twenty-seven hours that Sam Evans is no longer in Carrados?"

"Sam may not be that important. At least not to me, so I didn't notice he'd changed locations—if he did."

"Oh he did, and you know it because he called you from Kennedy."

"I tell you—"

"No, let me tell you," Maxvil interrupted, and his voice had a sharp edge to it now. "Sam Evans conveyed certain information to Mr. Styles. He had called you, he said. He had found out things in Carrados about Richard Potter that shook him up. The only person he knew to turn to was you. He'd always trusted you. He then said that if you turned out to be one of the bad guys instead of one of the good guys he was going to

93

be in big trouble. Then he would need help from Mr. Styles. If he didn't check back within twenty-four hours the big trouble had happened. It's now about twenty-seven hours, Mr. Zorn, and Sam Evans hasn't checked back. So it would seem you turned out to be one of the bad guys."

"That is pure, unadulterated crap," Zorn said. He looked at Peter. "And just what kind of help was Styles supposed to be able to give Sam?"

"Most potent weapon there is against your kind of people, Mr. Zorn," Maxvil said, sounding almost cheerful again. "World-wide publicity, the story from top to bottom under a respected byline. And I'm not just talking about a murder and a fire on Greenwich Avenue, Mr. Zorn. I'm talking about Richard Potter, what really happened to him and what's actually being done for him. I'm talking about the disappearance of Potter's girl and Potter's top assistant, Sam Evans. Peter, here, can make a story out of that material, Mr. Zorn, that will take the Middle East crisis right off the front pages and put Harkness Chemical and Latin American shenanigans right up front. Now you have a choice."

"What are you talking about—choice?"

"You can play dumb or you can cooperate," Maxvil said. "You can insist you never heard from Sam Evans, didn't know he was in this country, don't have any idea what has happened to Lynn Mason. Do that and no one, not Harkness Chemical with all its influence, not the State Department or the CIA, not the terrorist geniuses in Latin America, can stop Peter from stripping the lot of you naked, in public. That's one option you have, Mr. Zorn."

"There's another?" Zorn asked quietly. The ash from his cigarette dribbled down on his hairy chest. He didn't seem to notice it.

"You're a professional and a good one," Maxvil said. "Harkness wouldn't have you in charge of their security if you

94

weren't. You're following orders. You must have certain decision-making authority. You can't run to the chairman of the board every time you're faced with an action decision. So that's where you are now, Mr. Zorn. Faced with a decision. The Potter kidnapping is outside my department. That's Federal, International, Diplomatic. But the murder on Greenwich Avenue is mine, and the disappearance of people connected with it is mine. I want Hadley. I want Sam Evans if he isn't in the morgue, and if he is I want him identified. If the murdered man isn't either Evans or Hadley I want to know who he is. And finally, Mr. Zorn," Maxvil said, and glanced at his wristwatch, "I want to have breakfast with an alive and healthy Lynn Mason. Produce all those things for me and a reasonable excuse for still keeping the Potter case under a blanket and then, perhaps, Peter can persuade his managing editor not to plaster you on every front page all over the world." Maxvil smiled. "It's a simple alternative, Mr. Zorn."

Zorn took a deep drag on his cigarette and went into another coughing fit.

"Let me add something, Mr. Zorn," Maxvil said. "Peter Styles is one man. Don't ask yourself how he can be silenced. Because if anything happens to him, someone else will move into his place. And if anything happens to a top reporter like Peter Styles, the whole press corps, all over the world, will rise up to nail the people responsible. You must know blackmail when you see it, Zorn. You people at Harkness are experts at it. It's kind of a way of life with you, isn't it?"

Zorn reached out and crushed the stub of his cigarette against the wooden table top. There was no ashtray in the bare room.

"There are certain policy decisions I can't make, Lieutenant," he said, in his husky voice. This wasn't a frightened man. This was a coolly calculating man. Behind him, Peter knew, were literally billions of dollars worth of power, governments, agencies, his own security force. Aligned against this he and Maxvill must look like irritating pigmies to Zorn. But the irritation could be galling.

"I can't meet some of your requirements," Zorn said. "To start with, I had no idea that the Mason girl was missing till you told me. I don't know what's happened to her or where she is. I can't produce her for breakfast."

"Perhaps you can find her by breakfast time," Maxvil said. "You must know who wants her out of the way."

"I can try," Zorn said. "The odds aren't good, because she doesn't fit into my picture."

"Not even with the information that Potter is being held here, in the United States?"

"That's nonsense. He's in South America somewhere."

It was interesting, Peter thought. You listened and some things sounded true and some things didn't. He had the feeling that Zorn really didn't know what had happened to Lynn Mason, but that he very much wanted to find out. Peter also sensed that Zorn knew perfectly well that Potter wasn't in South America. He told the truth in a matter-of-fact way, he lied with a kind of urgency.

"I'll level with you on something else," Zorn said. "Sam Evans did call me from Kennedy night before last."

"So you did know he was back here," Maxvil said.

"Yes. He made an appointment to come directly here from the airport. He said he had new stuff on the Potter case."

"And did he?"

"He never came," Zorn said. "I waited here and then I got the news on the radio about the fire in the village. I didn't know what to think. The dead man could be Wilfred Hadley. It was possible that Sam had dropped off there—to leave his luggage, say—and that something happened to him."

"He accused Hadley of something and Hadley killed him?" Maxvil suggested.

96

"That occurred to me," Zorn said. "But there was no way I or any of my people could get information. You had the place beautifully shut off, Lieutenant."

"But you knew Hadley wasn't the dead man as the news suggested?"

"I knew because you brought in his dentist. The dentist is part of the Harkness medical setup. He reported to me that it wasn't Hadley. Just doing his job."

"So it is Evans," Maxvil said.

"I don't know," Zorn said. "Sam Evans is a very rare man. He had no dental problems so there is no dental chart in the company files."

"Who else could it be?"

"No notion," Zorn said. "But I will tell you this, Lieutenant. I have a pretty good staff of people working for me. We haven't been able to locate Hadley. Until night before last he's been in constant touch with us. Since then, nothing. And there's been nothing from Sam Evans to account for his failure to show up here."

"You must have tried to find the taxi he took from the airport," Maxvil said.

"We did. We found it. The driver took him to Lynn Mason's apartment on Jane Street."

Lynn hadn't been there, Peter knew. She'd been singing at the Greenwich Corner and he'd been there, listening.

"No trail after that," Zorn said. "If the girl was there, she may know where he was headed. Frankly, by the time we'd traced the taxi we weren't able to locate Lynn Mason. That was the next day after the fire."

"I can tell you that she didn't see Evans," Peter said.

Zorn heaved his big shoulders. "So that's the way it is, Lieutenant. If I wanted to tell you, I don't know where Hadley is; I don't know if Evans was the dead man in the fire, and if he wasn't, I don't know who the dead man is or where Evans is.

97

I can't produce the girl for breakfast or meet your other demands. Not that I haven't been working to find those answers. Not that I won't keep working to find them for my own purposes. Harkness wants those answers."

"You don't leave us much choice," Maxvil said. "Peter starts asking public questions that you may find embarrassing. Where is Potter? What is Harkness doing to free him? Four months have gone by. Where are two key men in your organization who have apparently disappeared? What has happened to a girl who was trying to find answers to those questions?"

"Let me argue against that course," Zorn said. "If you care about Potter, if you care about these other people, keep the lid on. Get on the trail and the people who've got them will make sure they aren't able to talk."

"What people?"

"The terrorists, of course," Zorn said. "They aren't some piddling little group of South American radicals. They're international, Lieutenant. They sway governments. They don't give a damn for individual human lives."

"Are you trying to say that whatever happens we're not likely to see Potter, or Hadley, or Evans, or Lynn Mason alive again?" Peter asked. His mouth felt dry.

"Unless Harkness, and the CIA, and the other big multinationals can come up with a deal," Zorn said. "Give them a chance, gentlemen, by not stirring the stew. That's the one chance your friends and my people have."

"What kind of a deal?"

"Not my department," Zorn said. His lined face hardened. "I think I might persuade Robert Harkness, the president of the corporation, or Cal Trevor, the executive vice-president in general charge, to talk to you. Later this morning. They may or may not give you a better argument than I can. It's their baby. I'm just a bodyguard."

"Is there a terrorist headquarters here in the city, or in the

98

eastern part of the country?" Maxvil said.

Zorn looked at the detective as if he was a not very bright child. "They are everywhere, Lieutenant, as you ought to know. But if you're asking for an address or a telephone number I can't help you."

A kind of exasperation overtook Peter. "You're suggesting something that I can't buy, Mr. Zorn," he said. "Keep the lid on! We're to sit home and do needlepoint while the lives of four people depend on whether politicians and corporations can make some kind of deal. I can sit on the story as far as publication is concerned, but I can't sit still. I have to be in motion toward finding those people. I can keep the lid on, as you put it, only as long as I'm headed somewhere."

"I've told you, we're as anxious as you are for answers," Zorn said. "My organization is doing everything it can to find answers. I have a man looking for Hadley out in Minnesota. That's where he came from originally. I thought he'd gone out there to visit family or friends. It was just possible he hadn't heard about the fire in which he was supposed to have died. But so far, nothing. No one who knows him out there admits to seeing him recently. I've told you, I've done everything I can to locate Sam Evans. So far the trail ends with the taxi driver who took him to Lynn Mason's apartment. The girl herself I don't know about. I've had a man looking for her to ask her about Evans, but we've drawn a blank there, too. Maybe I should be asking you for help instead of the other way around."

"You haven't mentioned Potter," Peter said.

Zorn made an impatient gesture with his big hands. "I've never bought the theory that he's in this country," he said. "Never mind the so-called code message to the girl. He was kidnapped in Carrados. Why would the terrorists ship him back here? It doesn't make sense. But I haven't ignored it. My people in Carrados have done everything they could to find a shred of evidence that would back up the idea. There's nothing. Not a rumor, not a bit of gossip."

"There's something missing, you know," Peter said. "I've read the original accounts and I've talked to Weldon Keach, the pilot who flew Potter to Carrados. They watched Potter get off the plane, walk across the airstrip and into the terminal building. But there's no account of what happened then. It seems that no one in the terminal saw anything unusual happen. No account of any violence. He vanished in the middle of a crowd of people." Peter glanced at Maxvil. "Just like Lynn at the Beaumont. It couldn't happen without anyone seeing something out of order, but it did."

"Somebody sticks a gun in your back in a place like Carrados and you don't argue," Zorn said. "Potter knew the place, knew the terrorist climate that's part of the place. He's a man with experience in what you might call violent politics. He wouldn't try to fight or escape with a gun in his ribs—any more than a sensible person would fight off a mugger in the back streets of this city. Potter was too experienced to go against impossible odds."

"Do you believe that Harkness Chemical can still make a deal for his release?" Peter asked. "Do you really believe that they are still trying to make a deal?"

"I'm told by the people I work for that they are," Zorn said.

"But at not too great a cost," Peter said. "Not at the cost of expropriation by the Carrados government."

"But good enough for the terrorists to keep Potter alive," Zorn said. "He was alive a week or so ago, you know. He answered questions that only he could answer."

"And then Perrault's people killed the man who brought the answers," Peter said.

"Some stupid bastard thought he could beat information out of the terrorist messenger," Zorn said. "It will cost plenty in whatever the deal turns out to be."

"If there is a deal," Peter said. "I think I'd like to take you

100

up on your offer, Zorn. I think I'd like to talk to someone at the top—Robert Harkness, the other man you mentioned, is it Cal Trevor?"

"Calvin Trevor," Zorn said. "He's a lot closer to the action than the Old Man. Call me at my office a little after nine tomorrow morning. I'll have set it up by then."

"We're running out of time," Peter said.

Zorn gave him a bitter little smile that suggested contempt. "You don't really care about human lives any more than anyone else, do you, Styles? Anything for a headline."

3

Out on the street Peter and Maxvil walked toward the avenue in search of a cab. They had skirted around the key question with Zorn. Sam Evans had told his friend Willis that he may have found out that the brass at Harkness was playing along with the terrorists. It hadn't been possible to ask a direct question or to hint at it. If Zorn was part of such a conspiracy, to let him know they suspected it would have put him on guard without any ammunition to strike with.

Much of what Zorn had told them could be the truth. Once the security man had gotten round to it his account of the call from Sam Evans and then Evans's failure to show could be for real. Checking the taxi driver who may have driven Evans to Lynn's apartment could be for real.

"But it could be only part of the truth," Peter said. "The man lies, if he was lying, with the same glibness that he tells the truth."

"Goes with the job," Maxvil said.

Evans had made it clear to David Willis that Zorn was a question mark. The security man could be on Evans's side or he could be the enemy. If Zorn was Evans's friend would he help unmask a conspiracy between his employers and the terrorists, or would he protect those employers no matter what the

102

cost to his friend Evans?

"I buy the taxi," Maxvil said. "We can and will double check it. That gets Evans as far as Lynn Mason's apartment. Who knows after that? According to Zorn, Evans said he was heading to Zorn's apartment straight from Kennedy. Why, if that's true, did he stop—out of his way—at Lynn Mason's?"

"To get a second person prepared to help him in case things went wrong," Maxvil suggested. "Perhaps to tell her something he'd found out about Potter. 'The girl was right,' he told Willis. Perhaps he meant to tell her how he knew she was right."

"And then he decides to drop his luggage at his own apartment, which is only a couple of blocks away."

"Or that's where Zorn starts to lie," Maxvil said. "Evans's apartment was where he agreed to meet Evans. He has guessed what Evans is going to tell him. Evans, friend or not, has to be silenced. Zorn would prefer to handle the silencing at Evans's place rather than his own."

The two men looked at each other.

"So Evans is murdered and burned," Peter said.

"Or Zorn is telling the truth," Maxvil said. "Evans did stop off to leave his luggage on his way to Zorn's and someone else took care of the silencing. You pays your money and you takes your choice. My job is to identify that corpse, then we'll know better what we're talking about."

"Do you have any doubts?" Peter asked.

"No," Maxvil said. "So watch your step. If Zorn takes you to the mountain top, play it cool. Let the Harknesses and the Trevors know you suspect something and you may find yourself in the shredding machine."

Back in his apartment Peter saw that David Willis had put quite a dent in the bourbon bottle.

"I was just about to go home in spite of your instructions," Willis said. "I keep having the feeling Sam may be trying to reach me."

"I don't think so," Peter said. "Any phone calls here?" He, too, was waiting to hear, without much hope. If Evans was the dead man then Maxvil's theory that Lynn might have seen him at the Beaumont was exploded. Evans had been dead long before that.

"No calls," Willis said. "I'm afraid I was rather generous with your booze, Mr. Styles."

Peter let him have it. There was almost no doubt that Evans was the victim in the Greenwich Avenue fire. Willis looked stunned.

"We need to be able to prove or disprove it, David," Peter said. "You went to school with Evans, you said."

"School and college."

"Where?"

"Hotchkiss and Yale."

"There must be family, friends, school doctors, college doctors who might be able to help us identify what's left of Evans. Sit down at my desk there and give me a list of such people."

"Oh God, Mr. Styles, did I wait too long to call you? If I'd called earlier would it have—?"

"No way," Peter said. "If we're right about this, Evans was killed not more than an hour or so after he talked to you."

"So Zorn turned out to be a bad guy?"

Peter shrugged. "Maybe, maybe not," he said.

Good guy or bad guy, Zorn kept his word about arranging an appointment for Peter with the top brass at Harkness Chemical. At ten minutes past nine he told Peter on the phone that he would be received at any time he arrived during the morning.

"In half an hour," Peter told him.

Tensions had mounted in Peter. There had been no word from Lynn. Maxvil's earlier theory that she had gone off of her own volition didn't stack up any more. At least he had to

104

believe that she was no longer free to communicate or she would have.

Maxvil had been busy while Peter had taken another short nap, waiting to hear from Zorn. A messenger from police headquarters brought Peter a manila envelope from the detective containing a copy of a police-artist's sketch of the man who'd been beaten and thrown down the fire stairs at the Beaumont, based on a description by Jerry Dodd. The thin bearded face with deep-set dark eyes suggested an intellectual rather than a man of violence. Maxvil had attached a note. *"Nothing on the fingerprints, either here or at the FBI. The man doesn't have a criminal record we know of."* Could he have any connection with Lynn's disappearance? He'd been in the hotel, asking for Peter, while he and Lynn had been upstairs in Walter Franklin's suite. He had been on the scene. He could have been involved, or seen something, or known something. Would he talk when the time came that he could talk?

The Harkness Building is a great steel and glass tower pointing to the sky in midtown Manhattan. The ground floor, visible from the street through giant glass panels, looked almost like a glamorous travel agency. There were huge mural paintings of Harkness operations in the Middle East, in Europe, in Carrados, and in the western United States. A small army of pretty girls wearing pale blue military-style jackets and skirts held forth at desks and counters. If you cared to ask questions they were answered by these brightly smiling dolls, you were handed folders describing what Harkness did to benefit the whole world. The greatest cancer research program in the country was conducted by Harkness scientists. Everyday drugs used to fight everything from the common cold to hay fever to colonic disturbances to heart ailments were produced by Harkness. Vaccines to fight polio and measles and diabetes and esoteric flu germs were part of their work. Harkness, you could discover, was a world benefactor. There were giant photographs of Harkness scientists dealing with famine-ravaged black children in South Africa and India. The smiling, uniformed girls sold Harkness to the general public from morning till night. How wonderful that a great American corporation did so much good for the common man, the disadvantaged people of the world.

What was not shown in this glassed-in showcase of corporate benevolence was information on other Harkness products. There were poison gases that could be used to wipe out whole communities, cities, and towns. There were variations on napalm which could defoliate whole forests and jungles. There were explosives powerful enough to blow up an airport or a rail terminal or waterfront docks, packaged so expertly that one man could carry death for a thousand men in the side pocket of his topcoat. This aspect of Harkness was not so benevolent and not advertised by the smiling girls. They would tell you about medicines, and about beauty creams and skin care lotions. The instruments of death were only talked about on upper floors which couldn't be reached without very careful scrutiny by an army of security people.

Peter discovered this when he asked for Gabriel Zorn. He was taken to an inner office where he was asked about his business. A phone call was made to Zorn who evidently cleared him. That wasn't quite enough. He was asked to reveal the contents of a brown manila envelope he was carrying. It contained the pencil drawing of the injured man in Bellevue and a four-month-old copy of *Newsview* magazine. Harmless enough, apparently. Then as he started to leave this first office he was stopped abruptly. He had passed through the beam of an electronic eye which revealed the fact that he was carrying a gun. Much excitement. Another call to Zorn who still cleared him. His gun was taken with notice that he could have it back when he left.

Zorn's office on the forty-first floor was not very unlike Max-

106

vil's guess about it; maps, charts, name boards. There were ticker-tape machines spouting news from the big services around the world. There were computers flashing meaningless numbers and symbols on screens, meaningless at least to Peter. There was a switchboard marked OVERSEAS at which operators seemed to be constantly busy.

This was the outer office. Zorn's inner office was almost as bare as the living room of his apartment. There was an intercom box on a bare desk, four telephone instruments each a different color, and on the wall opposite the desk was a screen, blank now, but, Peter guessed, ready to come alive with numbers, symbols, news items, computerized answers to any questions the man at the desk chose to ask. Peter had the feeling that he was looking at something almost unbelievable. In this electronic maze you could press a button and a man on a back street in Hong Kong would be instantly struck down. Peter had the absurd impulse to ask Zorn to press a button and get the answers he needed. Where is Lynn? Where is Hadley? Who is the man wrapped in bandages at Bellevue? Who killed Cock Robin?

Zorn presented a very different front than he had a few hours back. The rugged old man, bare chested, barefooted, aiming a gun at Maxvil, was replaced by a well-tailored, suave-looking bank president.

"Sorry about the gun," Zorn said. "I didn't dream you carried one or I'd have warned you."

"Your security seems to work," Peter said.

"I'm curious about the drawing you are carrying in that envelope," Zorn said. Everything got to him.

"I brought it for you to look at," Peter said. He took the drawing out of the envelope and put it on the desk in front of Zorn. "A police-artist sketch of a man who was asking for me at the Hotel Beaumont last night. He was later beaten half to death—about the time Lynn Mason disappeared."

Zorn stared at the drawing, a scowl wrinkling his forehead.

107

The cigarette he was smoking brought on a coughing fit and he put it out in a brass ashtray on his desk.

"Looks like some movie actor I've seen somewhere," he finally said. "I can put it through a computer for you. We have thousands of photographs on file. Might match up."

"This is only a copy," Peter said. "Easy enough for me to get another."

Zorn gave him that twisted smile. "You don't trust me, do you, Styles?"

"I wish I thought I could," Peter said. "But go ahead. See what your computer comes up with."

"We should have an answer when we come back down," Zorn said. He stood up.

Instantly the office door opened and a young man came in. A hidden button must have summoned him. Zorn handed him the drawing with instructions to "run it through."

"Back down?" Peter asked him.

"The Old Man—Robert Harkness—and Cal Trevor are waiting for you in the penthouse," Zorn said.

A private elevator took them to the very top of the building. They stepped off it into a small vestibule where they were confronted by a white-coated houseman. They were led across what looked like a small ballroom to an outdoor terrace. Two men were seated at an iron table with a glass top, a coffee service in front of them. They both rose as Zorn took Peter toward them.

The older of the two, probably Robert Harkness, had thick white hair, a ruddy face, and ice-blue eyes shaded by thick black eyebrows. He was a rugged version of his daughter, Frances Potter. A once-powerful body was draped in a white linen suit. He was wearing a salmon-pink shirt with a dark blue tie. A man used to commanding, Peter thought. He would have been the inspiring general in his time, leading the charge on his white horse. Peter had gleaned a few facts about Robert Harkness in

108

the first story about the Potter kidnapping which he carried in the envelope. This Robert Harkness was the son of the founder of the firm, a small manufacturer of pharmaceuticals. Robert Harkness had expanded his father's small family business into an empire. After forty years he was still president of the company, but its day-to-day operation had been taken over by younger men.

At the top of the echelon of younger men was Calvin Trevor, standing next to the "Old Man" as Zorn introduced Peter. Harkness gave Peter a brisk, impersonal nod, his blue eyes hostile. Trevor held out his hand, his smile cordial. His handshake was firm. He was dark, his hair styled modishly long, his clothes very mod.

"Gabe has filled us in pretty well with what's on your mind, Mr. Styles," Trevor said. "Sit down, won't you? Help yourself to coffee."

The sweet smell of flowers from boxes placed all around the terrace rail was almost overpowering.

"I don't understand why we have to justify our actions to you, Styles," Harkness said. "I would have told you to go jump in the lake, but Cal and Gabe seem to think we should listen to you."

"I'm here to listen to you," Peter said. "We're faced with an accumulation of violence. Your son-in-law is kidnapped; another of your people, Sam Evans, has disappeared and has probably been murdered; another of your men, Wilfred Hadley, vanishes; your son-in-law's girl friend disappears; another man, unidentified but somehow connected with it all, is brutally beaten and may not survive. I see all this and I am told by Mr. Zorn 'not to stir the stew,' to keep the lid on this while you make some kind of a deal for the release of Richard Potter, a deal that has been cooking for more than four months. We've kept the lid on as long as we can, gentlemen, without understanding exactly what you're up to. Negotiating for the release of Richard Potter is one thing; standing by while murder, and attempted murder, and abductions, and disappearances are added to the picture is too much to expect of us."

"We're involved in very delicate negotiations for a man's life," Harkness said. "The details of that negotiation are nobody's business."

"Meanwhile four other people are swept under the rug," Peter said, "dead, dying, held prisoner, or eliminated in some fashion we don't know about yet. Is that all part of the price for your son-in-law's freedom, Mr. Harkness?"

"We have no connection with those four people," Harkness said, his voice rising. "I'm talking about ourselves as negotiators. Hadley is our man. Evans is our man. But they're no part of the negotiating effort. Evidently they tried, without orders or instructions from us, to inject themselves into the situation and someone, not us, has objected to that interference and attempted to put an end to it. Richard's little sex queen"— and Harkness made that sound very nasty—"brought you into the picture, Styles, and the objectors have put an end to that. I don't know who your unidentified man is, but he, too, must have stuck his nose in where someone didn't want it. And this isn't a threat, Styles, but you could very well be next. If you stupid people who don't understand the whole pitch keep trying to wedge your way in, you may get the works, and our chances of effecting Richard's release may disappear. Why, for Christ sake, don't you mind your own damned business, Styles?"

"The truth about crime is my business," Peter said quietly. "Would you care to tell me who these 'someones' are who object so violently to people looking for facts?"

"Don't play babe-in-the-woods with me, Styles," Harkness said. "The terrorists, of course. They won't stand for people prying into their affairs. We know that here at Harkness. Our one chance of getting Richard free is to deal with them in good faith. Hadley and Evans, our people, knew this. They had

110

received a general directive from Trevor, our executive vice-president in charge, warning all Harkness employees to stay clear while the negotiations are in progress. They had received personal briefings from Cal, since they were both closely involved—Hadley who made the first response to the kidnappers' demands, Evans who was Richard's assistant. Evans clearly violated those instructions, by going to Carrados without permission, snooping around in God knows what cesspool. What Hadley was up to we won't know till we find him—if we find him. The terrorists, who have a worldwide espionage system better than any I know of, know what's happening minute to minute. They've acted."

"Is their system better than the one I saw downstairs in Zorn's office?" Peter asked.

"Better," Calvin Trevor said. He seemed to be waiting for the right moment to get into the act.

"The girl may not have been warned, but she should have been," Harkness went on. "I don't know about your unknown man in the hospital. But I know about you, Styles." His voice shook with anger. "You were warned, the whole goddamned press, the radio, the TV, have been warned by people in the highest places in this country, to pull back while we tried to negotiate for a man's life. They have all acted in a responsible fashion until you suddenly decide to raise a stink! Why, Styles? What the hell is eating you?"

"I have facts that the rest of the press and media haven't got," Peter said. "You don't have a complaint against me, Mr. Harkness. I came here to give you the chance to persuade me not to release those facts to everyone else."

"If you do start a media avalanche against us, you will have murdered Richard Potter," Harkness almost shouted.

Calvin Trevor chose his moment. "I think Mr. Styles has come here with a reasonable attitude, Bob," he said to the older man. His smile was ingratiating. "I have the feeling he isn't the

111

kind of man who likes to be threatened. Perhaps we should start over again."

"It's your ball game," Harkness said, and walked away toward the flower boxes from where he could look down over the city. Peter wondered how much of it he owned, how much of it he controlled.

"Coffee, Mr. Styles?" Trevor asked, still smiling.

Peter declined. All during this Gabriel Zorn stood off to one side, obviously choosing not to be a part of what was happening.

"It's difficult for anyone on the outside to understand exactly what is going on in Carrados," Trevor said. "It's more than just a political conflict in a small country. The terrorists aren't just involved with the government there. The whole South American continent is involved. The controversy between President Perrault's government, Harkness, and the terrorists is really just one segment of a struggle between many governments, literally hundreds of multinational corporations, and the terrorists all over Latin America. Democratic governments all over the world are concerned with the outcome, because that outcome will set a pattern for governments, big business, and the left not only in Latin America but in the Middle East, South Africa, and the entire Third World. We're not just negotiating for the release of Richard Potter but for a way of doing business which is vital not only to Harkness Chemical, but to business interests in the United States and all the industrialized democracies in the world. What we concede in this case can affect them all. We know this, the governments know it, and the terrorists know it. It would be hard for you to imagine the pressure that's being brought on us by our government, by other governments, and the whole big business community."

Harkness turned away from the flower boxes at the terrace rail. "Dick Potter is just a dummy in the store window," he said, still angry. "We're supposed to be negotiating for his

112

release, but in fact we're negotiating for the survival of an economic way of life."

"But you paid out three million dollars for Potter's release without a moment's hesitation when he was kidnapped," Peter said.

"Hadley acted without authority!" Harkness said.

Calvin Trevor shook his head slowly. "That isn't exactly the way it was, Bob," he said. "Hadley called me here in New York about the kidnapping and I told him to meet the demands. It appeared to Hadley, and I agreed, that it was simply an isolated violence. Then we came to see that it involved a great deal more than Potter."

"And you backed off," Peter said.

"We had no choice!" Harkness shouted from his position by the flower boxes.

"We had to consult with other multinationals," Trevor said, "with our government. We had to try to persuade President Perrault of Carrados that to seize Harkness assets would result in similar seizures all over the world and that he would go down the drain with us, the people he was trying to publicly punish for breaking his rules."

"Rules made after the fact!" Harkness said.

"Do you see at all, Mr. Styles, why you have to stay out of this?" Trevor asked. "You won't help the individual people you're concerned about. You won't help Dick Potter, or his girl, or Evans, or Hadley, or your man in the hospital."

"Someone's got to help them," Peter said.

"But not you, Mr. Styles. Not your way. Let me point out a fact of life to you. The media, which quite naturally likes to exploit stories of violence, unintentionally in most cases becomes the ally of terrorists all over the world. Blowing up this story at this moment of delicate negotiations is exactly what the terrorists would like. It makes their position look strong. If we concede anything to them at all, it makes us look weak. Little governments, like President Perrault's, can't afford to look weak or the people turn against them and the terrorists take over. The one way out of this predicament for everyone is to keep the story buried. Give us the chance to work out something. If you don't, you won't save anyone and you could throw whole populations into the hands of the terrorists. I promise you, Mr. Styles, it's not worth a headline."

Round and round you go and you come out nowhere, Peter thought. Trevor's argument had some basis in fact. It was why Devery and others in the media had held off for so long.

"But what becomes of Richard Potter and the others?" he asked. "Can the terrorists afford to set him free without getting important public concessions from Harkness and the Carrados government? Can they afford to look weak?"

"Let's be realists, Mr. Styles," Trevor said. "I would say that Dick Potter's chances are very slight unless President Perrault weakens his stand on political prisoners."

"Potter is my son-in-law!" Harkness said. "Goddamn it, don't you think I'd pay anything to get him free? We've already paid millions. If more money was the answer, I'd find it. But money won't change Perrault's stand. A man will sell almost anything, but not his own neck. We're offering everything we can for Dick—and praying, for God sake!"

"What can you offer but money?" Peter asked.

Trevor spoke quickly before Harkness could reply. "That I can't tell you at the moment," he said. "Let us say, readjustments in the handling of our interests in Carrados. But to get back to the main point, Mr. Styles. Publicize the fact that Lynn Mason and possibly Hadley and Evans are in terrorists' hands and you place them in the same position as Dick Potter. Possible point of no return. I urge you, if you are concerned about them and not just some splashy headlines, back off. They may have a chance if you can resist the temptation of a big story."

Harkness came back across the terrace to stand in front of

Peter. "It seems to be your decision to make, Mr. Styles, not ours. You came to us to make demands. Cal is telling you what meeting those demands could cost."

"It's a matter of timing, Mr. Styles," Trevor said. "At some point you'll have your story, but what the story is may depend on your patience and your conscience."

David Willis's words kept going round in Peter's head as he and Zorn left the terrace. Sam Evans had told his friend that he may have found out that the top brass at Harkness Chemical were playing along with the terrorists. Walter Franklin, the State Department man, had suggested the same thing. The whole pious concern for Richard Potter and the others could be a fake. Big business could have decided that there would be more eventual profits in dealing with the terrorists than with the uncertain democratic-leaning governments. To accomplish this, however, victory must be made to look like defeat. It must appear that Harkness Chemical and the other multinationals in Latin America had been forced to their knees by the terrorists. No one must guess that this was the path to greater wealth, to greater power. There would be public mourning for the dead pawns in the game, Richard Potter, Sam Evans, Lynn Mason, possibly Wilfred Hadley and the man with no name in Bellevue Hospital. The heart-warming attempt by Harkness Chemical to negotiate for their safety would have failed. The whole game a cynical fraud.

That was the way it could be. But proof? Sam Evans must have discovered something and he was almost certainly dead. Lynn Mason must have learned something in those few moments at the Beaumont or why keep her silent? Hadley had disappeared so he must know something or be in on it. The man at Bellevue was not supposed to have survived his savage beating. Because he knew something? Proof must lie very close at hand. Lynn Mason had known nothing, Peter was certain, yet three minutes later in time it had been necessary to silence her. What had she seen? Who had she seen? If a clue to the truth was that close by, then it wasn't impossible that Peter could find it—the hole in the fence Maxvil had mentioned through which one man could go but not an army.

Back in Zorn's office Peter fought the urge to get out of this steel and glass fortress just as quickly as he could. He had the feeling that the slightest indication that he hadn't bought the bill of goods that Trevor and Harkness had tried to sell him could result in his never finding his way out onto the sunlit streets of the city again.

Zorn, his face the pleasant bank president's mask, made no comment on the terrace interview. He didn't ask Peter if he had understood. Peter had the feeling that Zorn had arrived at an answer to that. He hoped to God it was the wrong one.

"Let's see what the computer tells us about your picture," Zorn said.

For the second time the young man appeared as if pressing a button could materialize him in the office. He put the pencil drawing down on Zorn's desk.

"Nothing that makes any sense," he said. "The closest we come is to the film actor, Paul Newman, wearing a beard and mustache. Newman is very much alive and well and making a film in London."

"I said it reminded me of a movie actor," Zorn said. He nodded to the young man, who was instantly gone. He leaned back in his chair and looked thoughtfully at Peter, who was putting the photograph of the drawing back in his manila envelope. "I'd like to make a guess," he said.

"Guess?"

"At your next move," Zorn said. "Perhaps you don't publish the story, but I'm dead sure you don't quit. You feel responsible for the girl. Being a romantic you won't just sit back and twiddle your thumbs."

116

"And you're warning me not to be an idiot?"

"I'm wondering what I would do in your place," Zorn said. "I spend a good part of my time wondering what I would do in another man's shoes. If he's a clever man like you, Styles, I often come up with answers." He smiled. "The most difficult people to guess about are stupid people."

"So what would you do in my shoes?" Peter asked. He had tucked the brown envelope under his arm. He was ready to go.

"If I were in your shoes," Zorn said, "I would start at square one."

"Which is?"

"Where it all began," Zorn said. "The flight that took Dick Potter from Kennedy to Carrados. There were three poeple on that flight with Potter: Weldon Keach, the pilot whom you've met; George Connors, the copilot and navigator; and Marcia Lewis, the stewardess. Keach probably won't be cooperative with you after your visit with him. The other two might tell you things. Did Potter sleep on the trip? Did he eat well? Did he communicate with anyone on the plane's radio?"

"What would the answers to those questions get me?"

Zorn shrugged. "Who knows? In your shoes I'd feel I had to begin somewhere." He stood up. "My advice to you would be to forget it, but since you won't, I suggest square one. One thing you can do for me."

"Oh?"

"As soon as your friend Maxvil is officially certain that the dead man in the fire is Sam Evans I'd appreciate knowing it." A little nerve twitched in his cheek. "Sam was a good man, and he was my friend."

"If Maxvil agrees," Peter said.

Zorn sank back into his chair like a man who was tired. "Don't forget your gun," he said. "You may find you have a need for it—at some point."

117

4

There was no problem about the gun. The guards on the main floor returned it to Peter without question, and he found himself out on the street, fighting the impulse to run, to get as far away from the Harkness Building as quickly as he could. A block away he turned back and looked at it, up at the glittering spire at the very top. Just below that spire Harkness and Trevor might still be discussing his visit and wondering if they had won or lost. Peter had the feeling that they must have decided they'd won, or he wouldn't be out here, free and unhampered.

The Newsview Building was only a block away and Devery was there in his office. Devery was an angry man.

"You'd hardly gotten over there, Peter, when I got the word from high places. No story until I get clearance. I've been in this business thirty years, and no government official has ever tried to tell me what I can print and what I can't."

"And you have to obey orders?" Peter asked.

"The argument was persuasive," Devery said. "But when the sonsofbitches try to make it an order—!"

"I heard a persuasive argument, too," Peter said. He described his interview at the Harkness penthouse.

"And you bought it?" Devery asked, when Peter finished.

"I don't think so," Peter said. "But I'm inclined to hold off all the same. Would you believe I was offered some help by Gabriel Zorn?"

"No," Devery said, "I wouldn't."

"He suggested something that doesn't make much sense, and yet I have the curious feeling it may be worth trying." Peter went into Zorn's suggestion about "square one."

"Whether he slept, what he ate, whether he made a radiophone call?" Devery sounded angrier. "He's just trying to send you on some kind of a wild goose chase, keep you busy doing the wrong things. Keach won't talk to you. The copilot and the stewardess belong to Harkness. What could they tell you and what would they tell you if they could?"

"I had a feeling Zorn was trying to level with me in some fashion."

"Level with you?" Devery's laugh was short and mirthless. "Zorn is an expert at the double cross. That's why he's got the job he's got. They tried to sell you on keeping the story buried and now they're trying to keep you busy chasing nothings! Whether he slept and what he ate! That ought to fascinate our readers!"

"I'd like to make sure," Peter said. "Something about the way Zorn spoke of Sam Evans as his friend— I'd like to make sure he was just trying to keep me occupied out of the firing zone. There aren't any other arrows pointed in any other direction, Frank."

Two small jet planes were housed in a private hangar at Kennedy belonging to Harkness Chemical. Peter had not wanted to advertise his coming and he'd expected it would take some time for him to make contact with and locate George Connors, the copilot, and Marcia Lewis, the stewardess. By what at first seemed like a great piece of good luck he found them both standing by in the Harkness hangar. Some big shot in the company, Peter was told, was planning a trip to the West

Coast, time uncertain. Crew was to stand by. Connors was to be the pilot this time, a young copilot was also present. They wore pale blue uniforms like the girls in the lobby of the Harkness Building.

They were attractive young people, Connors and Marcia Lewis. He was a tall blond with an easy smile, she a trim, very pretty girl with natural red hair, and wide grey-green eyes. They were both the kind of young people you'd expect to find on a corporation payroll, alert, probably more than competent at their jobs.

Peter had asked for them at a small front office and been told they were in the "lounge room" just beyond. He had been surprised to find them so readily available, surprised and grateful.

"It's fun to meet you, Mr. Styles," Marcia Lewis said. She had a nice firm, one-of-the-boys handshakes. "I've been reading your things in *Newsview* ever since I can remember." Her eyes shadowed. She was remembering that the last pieces she had read had been about the death of his wife. She didn't mention them.

"I'm in luck to find you both here," Peter said. "I've some questions I want to ask you about the Potter case."

"Oh, brother!" Connors said. "We must have gone through that a dozen times—for the brass at Harkness, the CIA, the FBI, a man from the State Department. I'm not sure that as employees of Harkness we ought to talk to the press, Mr. Styles."

"Gabriel Zorn suggested that I try to find you," Peter said. "You read about the fire two nights ago in Greenwich Village? You may have noticed it because it involved Harkness employees."

"Mr. Hadley!" the girl said.

"And Sam Evans. It was Evans's apartment." Peter waited for a reaction but there was none. "What you don't know,

120

because the police haven't made it public yet, is that the man who was burned in the fire wasn't Hadley, and that he'd been shot through the heart before the fire was set. It was murder."

"Oh, man!" Connors said.

"We think the dead man is Evans. He'd been in Carrados and just gotten back an hour or so before it happened. We think he'd found out something about Potter and someone had to silence him before he could tell anyone what it was."

"The terrorists?" Marcia Lewis asked.

"Seems logical," Peter said. "There's more. Potter had a girl, not his wife."

"The Old Man must have blown his stack if he's heard that," Connors said.

"The girl has disappeared," Peter said, ignoring the comment. "It's a whole new ball game from my point of view. That's why I wanted to go back to the beginning, to ask you about the flight that took Richard Potter to Carrados." Peter opened his manila envelope and took out the picture the police artist had drawn of the man in Bellevue and the back issue of *Newsview* that contained the original kidnapping story. "This man may be dead as I talk to you," Peter said. "He was brutally beaten at a time he was looking for me, perhaps to tell me something."

Connors shook his head. "Never seen him," he said.

The girl agreed that the man was a stranger to her.

"It may not get me anywhere, but I'd like to get the story of Potter's flight to Carrados first hand. I didn't cover the story at the time. There could be more than's in the magazine story."

"There really isn't anything to tell," Connors said. "I mean, nothing unusual. Colonel Keach was to fly the plane."

"Colonel?"

"That was his military title in Vietnam. People still use it around here. He asked for me as copilot and navigator. I'd flown with him before and I'd made the Carrados run a couple

121

of dozen times. Marcia was to be the stewardess."

Marcia had picked up the magazine and was glancing at the original story. There are four stewardesses on the staff here," she said. "I wasn't asked for. It just happened to be my turn."

"We understood there were to be two passengers, Potter and Sam Evans," Connors said, "but Sam didn't make the flight."

"You knew Evans?"

"Sure. Flown him a dozen times with Potter to Carrados, to Europe, to Cairo."

"So you knew them both?"

"Sure. I mean, to say hello and pass the time of day. I wasn't friends with either of them," Connors said.

"Evans didn't make the flight. Overslept or something?"

"That's what he said afterwards, I heard. I had orders to taxi the plane out onto the runway ready for takeoff. We had a time, you understand. Then I got word from the control tower that our takeoff was to be delayed. I just waited. Finally Colonel Keach came into the pilot's compartment and told me we were ready when the word came from the tower. Potter was aboard. Evans hadn't made it."

"You saw Potter?"

"Not then. I was in touch with the tower trying to get clearance. As a matter of fact I never did see him until he left the plane at Carrados. He slept all the way, from all accounts."

Peter looked at Marcia who was frowning down at the old magazine story. "You were there when Colonel Keach brought his passenger aboard?" he asked.

"Mr. Potter? Well, not exactly," Marcia said. "There are two private compartments in these small jets. I went on board with George to make sure those two compartments were in order. We expected two passengers, you know. I made up the two bunks. It was a night flight and the chances were our passengers would sleep. There are also desks and dictating machines in case they want to work. One of the ground crew called me to

122

say I was wanted in the office. So I went."

"Something unusual?" Peter asked.

"No. There was mail to be delivered to the office in Carrados. When I say mail, I mean letters and some envelopes like this one." She nodded at Peter's manila job. "Not mail in the sense that it was post office stuff. But we often act as couriers for stuff the main office wants to go to wherever we're headed. There was quite a lot of it and I had to sign for each piece separately. When I got back to the plane Colonel Keach was already aboard and Mr. Potter was in one of the compartments. Colonel Keach told me he wasn't feeling well and didn't want to be disturbed. I wasn't to bother him unless he sent for me. He also told me that Mr. Evans wasn't making the trip."

"And did Potter ever send for you?"

"No," Marcia said. "When we were about to take off I knocked on his compartment door and told him we were taking off and to fasten his seat belt. He thanked me. I didn't check with him because he was an old hand on these flights."

"And he didn't call you at any time on the trip?"

"No." She looked rather strained, Peter thought. "When we were about to put down at Carrados I knocked on his door again and gave him the seat-belt warning. He thanked me again."

"So you saw him off the plane?"

"Not exactly," Marcia said. "Colonel Keach buzzed me and I went forward to the pilot's compartment. It was something about the mail I was to deliver. George was actually landing the plane. He set it down. A moment later Colonel Keach pointed to the window. 'There goes our boy,' he said, and I saw Mr. Potter walking across the airstrip to the terminal building."

"And it was Mr. Potter?"

"Who else?" Connors said. "The ground crew had wheeled up the steps to the plane and Potter let himself out. As Marcia said, he was an old hand at these trips."

123

"And that's it?" Peter asked. He could feel his pulse beating a little faster than normal. There was something about this story, if you had doubts, that made you wonder. But where next?

"He slept the whole way, then?" he asked.

"At least he made no demands," Marcia said. "No drinks, no sandwiches, no nothing."

"What do you do after you've landed at a place like Carrados?"

"Do?" Connors asked.

"About the plane?"

"Turn it over to the ground crew, with any instructions we may have for them. I don't remember that there was anything special on that occasion."

"So you go somewhere. Out through the terminal?"

"Yes. Colonel Keach and Marcia and I went out through the terminal."

"No excitement there?"

"Nothing. We never knew that anything had happened to Potter till we got back here to New York."

Peter had asked all the questions, indirectly, that Zorn had suggested but one. About sleep, about food Marcia had volunteered. He asked the last one.

"Do you recall if Potter made any kind of radio call from the plane to someone back here or up ahead in Carrados?" he asked.

"No. He didn't make any call."

"You'd know?"

"Of course," Connors said. "It would have to go through us in the pilot's compartment. We'd have to make the connection for him. People investigating have asked that question over and over."

That was that. Peter picked up his picture and his magazine and put them back in the manila folder. This story had been

124

told before, just as it had been told to him. Hadn't it occurred to anyone, specially after Lynn Mason had told her story about the code message indicating that Potter was in the United States, that Potter had never taken the trip to Carrados at all? Neither Connors nor Marcia Lewis had ever been face to face with the passenger. But of course there was a third witness who would have given investigators no reason to wonder. Colonel Weldon Keach, friend of Potter's family, had brought Potter aboard the plane himself. His testimony would make the rest of it seem normal enough. No one had had any reason to suspect. Was there really any reason to suspect now? Only that Zorn had sent him here. Was this what Zorn thought he might find?

Peter thanked the two young people and headed out toward an exit gate. He had gone about fifty yards when he heard hurried footsteps behind him. It was Marcia Lewis.

"Could I talk to you a minute, Mr. Styles?" She was breathless.

"Of course."

She looked directly at him and he thought he recognized fear. "I know Lynn Mason," she said. "Is it true she's disappeared?"

"It's true, Marcia."

"And you think—the same people who are involved in the other thing—?"

"That's what I think."

"I wish I knew what to do, Mr. Styles. I—I'm frightened."

"How can I help?"

"I think I can help you," she said. She reached out and grabbed his forearms. Her hands were shaking. "If these people mean to hurt Lynn—"

"If she knows what you know?" Peter suggested. "Let me guess. You know that the man you took to Carrados that night was not Potter?"

She nodded her head, vigorously. "I used to carry messages

125

from Dick Potter to Lynn. We'd take him on trips to different places and he'd give me notes to take back to her. They were terribly in love, those two."

"You saw the passenger that night?"

"It isn't that I saw him, Mr. Styles. But Dick Potter would have made a point of seeing me. He'd have had a message for Lynn. I even asked him when I knocked on the door as we were landing. Whoever it was didn't know what I was talking about!"

PART THREE

PART THREE

1

The girl still clung to Peter, and he could feel her fingernails biting through the sleeves of his summer jacket. He looked around. Ten to one his trip here was covered. Zorn had sent him. Zorn could easily have him observed. There were dozens of places from which he could be watched. No one had to be close by. They would know he had come here to meet Connors and the girl, and they would have seen her follow him out of the hangar.

"You never told anyone this before?" he asked the girl.

"No."

"Why not?"

"Because Colonel Keach was the chief witness," she said. "He made it quite clear he'd brought Dick Potter onto the plane. I—I was sure it wasn't Dick, but I never actually saw who it was."

"Walking across the airstrip from the plane?"

"His back was to us—it was only just daylight. It could have been Dick, except I was sure it wasn't."

"And you kept it to yourself until now?"

"I couldn't prove anything," she said. "If I'd called Colonel Keach a liar, just on the basis of a feeling I had, I'd have been in big trouble. When Lynn insisted, publicly, that Dick was

129

somewhere here in the United States, I didn't think I needed to get into the act. My job is important to me."

"You told Lynn you could back her up?"

"I didn't get a chance to," Marcia said. "Her story came out only eight or nine days ago. That's when they made it public that they were sure Dick was alive because of the way he'd answered the questions. I was on a trip to Tel Aviv. We were ferrying one of the big shots all over the Middle East. We didn't get back till yesterday. I read about the fire and all and I tried to call Lynn. I was never able to reach her." She backed away from him. "I've got to get back to the hangar. Our passenger may show up any minute."

"They can see you if they need you," Peter said. "Tell me what you can about Weldon Keach. You've flown with him before that night to Carrados?"

She gave him a bitter little smile. "Too many times," she said. "The colonel gets lonely when he's away from his home base."

"A sex king?"

She nodded. "When you're alone, in a strange place, in a strange country, with nothing to do—"

"You found him attractive?"

"I'm afraid I did. So did other girls who traveled with him. He—he plays the field."

"You liked him too much to contradict his testimony?"

"You don't cross top people in Harkness if you want to hang onto your job," Marcia said. She looked almost defiantly at Peter.

"But you've told me."

"Because if Lynn is in danger—"

"She's in danger," Peter said. "Now listen to me, Marcia. For your own safety, we haven't had this conversation. You followed me out here to ask about Lynn, your friend. If anyone asks you questions, stick to your original story. You had no reason to doubt that the passenger you carried that night was

130

Potter. I'm grateful to you, though. You've given me the first solid lead I've had."

"Lead?"

"Weldon Keach," Peter said. "I hope you're not so gone on him that you'll decide you have to tell him that you've talked to me."

"I'm not in favor these days," she said. "There is a new girl he asks for on his flights." The bitter little smile still twisted her mouth.

"This is no kind of situation in which to get even, or even get honest," Peter said. "There is so much money at stake, one way or the other, that if you upset the wrong people you can't expect any mercy."

"And you?" she asked.

"God knows who's playing what games," he said, "but there's one person who doesn't deserve to get hurt. Lynn asked me for help. I'm going to try to find a way. How can I reach you, Marcia, if I need to?"

"Phone book," she said. "Weldon Keach can be very tough if he's crossed."

"He's quite a few rungs down the ladder from the top," Peter said. "It's the top ones who are really scary."

In a taxi back to the city Peter tried to put the pieces together. The answered questions from Potter had convinced Lynn that he was being held in the United States. Marcia Lewis's story made it clear that he had never left the country. The kidnapping had taken place here, on home soil. The fake passenger, so carefully arranged for by Keach, had been meant to focus attention in the wrong place. He hadn't missed a detail. He had known Connors would be in the pilot's compartment. He had arranged for Marcia to be called to the hangar for the "mail." Sending for her to join the pilot and the copilot as they landed in Carrados had allowed the fake Potter to leave the plane.

Keach had then called attention to the man walking away from the plane. "There goes our boy," Keach had said. Connors had no reason to doubt it, but Marcia had. Keach, dealing with people he thought he knew, hadn't been aware that Potter was in the habit of using Marcia to carry messages to Lynn. If he had he certainly wouldn't have had Marcia as the stewardess on that flight. The first and only slip in a well-thought-out plan. Even Sam Evans's story that he had been slipped a Mickey at a party had the ring of truth now. People had laughed and thought he was just covering the fact that he'd had too much to drink and passed out. Keach couldn't have allowed him to take the trip or none of it would have worked. The Mickey was for real.

Where had the party been? Evans couldn't be asked. Lynn had said she didn't know. Keach, or someone working for Keach, had been there to drug Evans's drink. How to get on the trail without Keach knowing too soon, before there was enough ammunition to sink him?

Every step in thinking about it brought you to a new question. It was difficult to imagine that Weldon Keach, the smiling young Clark Gable type, the woman chaser brazenly living with Dick Potter's wife, playing on the side with attractive stewardesses, was anything but a follower of orders. A clever one, an efficient one, but not a man who could juggle economic empires on his own. Keach was a soldier in an army, Peter was certain, with the general and his staff somewhere up the line. On the penthouse of the Harkness Building?

And then there came an unanswered question that threw it all out of gear. Peter would never have gone to Kennedy to look for Connors and Marcia Lewis without the suggestion from Gabriel Zorn. It had seemed very lucky to find the copilot and the stewardess in the Harkness hangar. Could their orders to be ready for a flight to the West Coast have been designed to have them there when Peter arrived? Could those orders have

132

come from Zorn? Had Zorn expected Peter to find just what he had found? If he knew what Peter would find why hadn't he acted on it himself? On what team was Zorn playing?

An unpleasant idea occurred to Peter as his taxi approached Manhattan. Was he being set up? Was this whole thing designed to send him off on Keach's trail, keep him busily headed along a false trail? Had Marcia been a good actress and not really a girl frightened for her friend? He wondered, grimly, if he had let himself be had. Was Keach just a mechanical rabbit set in motion to start him running his lungs out in the wrong direction? Had Zorn faked him out of his socks? And if he hadn't, what the hell was his game?

In the better than half day Peter has used on his visits to the Harkness Building and then to the airport, Maxvil had finally nailed down an important fact. The murdered man whose body had been burned in Sam Evans's apartment was Sam Evans. David Willis, Evans's friend, had come up with a doctor in New Haven who had performed a knee operation on Sam Evans following a football injury. A small metal disc had replaced a shattered kneecap, and that disc was in the charred remains in the medical examiner's possession. Not that Maxvil or Peter had doubted it after the first uncertainties. Now it was no longer a guess. Also, Maxvil had found the taxi driver who had taken Evans from Kennedy to Lynn Mason's address on the night Evans had returned from Carrados.

So one part of Gabriel Zorn's story checked out.

"But sending you to Kennedy to talk to those two?" Maxvil shrugged. "You're right, of course, ten to one they were there on orders from him—to make it convenient for you."

"So he knew what I'd find out—or what I'd imagine I'd found out," Peter said.

"A devious man," Maxvil said. He took a deep drag on his inevitable cigarette. "But somehow I don't buy the idea that he's sent you off on a wild goose chase, chum. You're aimed too directly at the center of things—Keach, Frances Potter who is Harkness's daughter. He could have given you a lead that would have sent you off to Carrados, or China for that matter, well out of the way. Instead he points you at the bosom of the family, Harkness's family. It doesn't make sense, but he could be hoping you'd help him with something he can't get at himself."

"All he has to do is press a button!" Peter said. "You should see that place."

"There are people to look for," Maxvil said. "Richard Potter, your girl Lynn, Wilfred Hadley. Any one of them could take us right to the bull's-eye. And there's a new one."

"The man who made the trip to Carrados in Potter's place," Peter said. "No kidnapping in Carrados, of course. The phoney Potter just walked into the terminal and evaporated into the crowd."

"And there was a party where a man was drugged," Maxvil said. "Surely that's the only explanation for Evans missing that plane. We just keep going round and round until we come up with a brass ring; and there must be half a dozen of them."

"Is there any way you can get at Keach?" Peter asked.

Maxvil shook his head. "Nothing to tie him to the murder, which is my department. Oh, I can ask him for information about Evans and get the man's life story. But if I, or you, or anyone hints to him that we're wondering if he didn't stage an elaborate fake on the Potter trip, he'll be off and gone before we have any legal basis to hold him. We need more solid proof than Marcia Lewis's story. Maybe it's all on the level. Maybe Potter was on that plane, in that compartment, and simply didn't want to be bothered with messages to Lynn."

"I just don't believe that," Peter said. "I've thought about it, and if Marcia Lewis was acting when she told me her story, then I'd better retire as an investigative reporter. You have to have a feeling for the truth, and I swear she was leveling with me."

"I'm inclined to agree," Maxvil said. "Now I suggest you do Zorn the favor he asked from you. Call him and let him know we've identified Evans. It'll be on the evening news anyway."

"And then?"

"And then, my friend, all you can do is follow your nose."

"Whatever happened to those listening ears of yours?" Peter asked his friend.

"Wrong ears, listening in the wrong places," Maxvil said. "From the start I believed your Miss Mason, but I assumed Potter had been brought back here from South America after the kidnapping. I've had people listening at the main airports, at private landing fields. Potter, according to all accounts, is a big man. You don't carry him around in a suitcase. It's not easy to move an unwilling man around in the public eye. Now we know I've been wasting time. Potter never left New York at all. The kidnapping took place here. He was locked away somewhere before anyone knew he was missing. He could be in any one of a million houses or apartments within a radius of twenty miles of this office."

"And Lynn could be in the same place," Peter said.

"If she is being held," Maxvil said. He sounded grim. "Too many hostages can get awkward. Keep your eye on Keach, Peter. He's the key, but don't frighten him off before we can develop some legal reason for holding him."

The cat-and-mouse game with Zorn was played out. Peter called him and gave him the official word on Sam Evans. For a moment there was the sound of anger in Zorn's voice.

"I was afraid of that," he said. "Sam was a good man. These bastards play tough."

"Which bastards, Zorn?" Peter asked.

"Why, the terrorists, of course," Zorn said, and he was the

135

smooth-sounding bank president again. "I understand you took the trip to Kennedy. Was it worth while?"

"I want to thank you for having Connors and the Lewis girl waiting for me," Peter said.

Zorn chuckled. "Was it that obvious? I must be losing my touch. Was it worthwhile?"

"I don't suppose I found out anything you don't already know," Peter said. "The same old details about Potter's flight to Carrados."

Zorn sounded genuinely disappointed. "I hoped someone might tell you something they held back from me, or cops, or CIA people. Well, you can only try. Sorry if it was a waste of time."

The man was a puzzle. Was he laughing at Peter, there in his little bare office at Harkness Chemical? Was he involved in some game of his own in which he thought Peter could have been really helpful? Did he know exactly what Marcia Lewis had told Peter and exactly where it would lead him?

There was just one person outside Devery and Maxvil whom Peter felt he could trust. He had some difficulty locating Walter Franklin, the State Department man. After nearly an hour, waiting at the telephone in his apartment, a paging service at the United Nations got Franklin through to Peter.

"Something new, Mr. Styles?" Franklin asked.

"I need information," Peter said, "and I don't want anyone, particularly anyone at Harkness Chemical, to know I'm asking for it."

"I'll do what I can," Franklin said.

"I want a dossier on a man named Weldon Keach. He's a former colonel in the Air Force who works for Harkness."

"Ah, yes. The pilot who flew Richard Potter to Carrados."

"That's the man. I want everything there is to know about him. If the FBI has a file on him, I'd like to see it. If the CIA has a file on him, I'd like that. If you have anything on him at

136

State, I'd like that. I want everything on him, where he went to school, his record in the service, his friends, how he got involved at Harkness. Any sidelights on him I haven't mentioned."

"And you want all this yesterday," Franklin said drily.

"Or sooner," Peter said. "Lives are at stake, Mr. Franklin. And, incidentally, it's now official. The murdered man in the fire in Greenwich Village was Sam Evans."

"I expected that," Franklin said. "How do I reach you?"

"I'd better get to you."

"Call me in an hour for preliminaries," Franklin said. "I should have something by then. Contrary to rumor, we can move pretty rapidly at State if someone lights a fire."

Peter had only just hung up his phone when it rang. The caller was Marcia Lewis.

"I hoped I'd find you in, Mr. Styles," she said.

He felt suddenly weary of the whole game, if it was a game. "You didn't go to the West Coast," he said.

"The flight was called off," she said. "Harkness executives change their minds as often as women."

"And you've changed your mind about what you told me?"

"No!" she said. "I want to bring a friend of mine to see you. He may be helpful. He's a newspaper man like you. South American. His name is Jaymie Santos. You may have heard of him."

Peter had seen the name. A freelance contributor to a dozen Latin American newspapers, as he recalled it. Santos had once sold Devery a special article on political upheavals in Argentina. This was a man who could know Carrados like the back of his hand.

"I'll be here for an hour," Peter said. "After that I can't promise where I'll be."

"We can get to you in twenty minutes," Marcia said.

It could be genuine help, it could be another false lead. He

137

had an hour to wait for Franklin's report. It was another hour in which the clock ticked away on Lynn Mason and Richard Potter. Nothing moved!

Marcia and her newspaper man made it in better than twenty minutes. Out of her crisp, blue, impersonal uniform and wearing a pale green summer cotton Marcia was rather special. Keach's interest in her as a sideline romance was quite understandable. Jaymie Santos, wearing a neatly tailored gabardine suit with a yellow sport shirt open at the throat, was slim, dark, with snapping black eyes and a wide, ingratiating white smile. He spoke English with a very slight accent—more a different inflection than an accent.

"It is an honor to meet you, Mr. Styles," he said.

"Jaymie is an old friend," Marcia said.

The way Santos smiled at the girl suggested to Peter that he had helped her to occupy her time "away from home with nothing to do."

"Make you a drink?" Peter asked.

Marcia wasn't interested but Santos looked eagerly at the little bar in the corner. Peter suggested he help himself. Marcia dropped down in a corner of the couch, handsome legs tucked up under her.

"It's a kind of coincidence that made me bring Jaymie here," she said. "Not twenty minutes after you left Kennedy, Mr. Styles, Jaymie turned up, asking almost the same questions you'd asked me."

"And you gave him the same answers?" Peter asked.

She nodded. "I thought he might be able to help us find Lynn," she said.

Santos came over from the bar, carrying a gin and tonic. "I, too, wondered," he said, "when Miss Mason's story about the code message broke—her insistence that Potter was here in the United States. I arrived from Carrados to look for Marcia. I simply couldn't believe that the terrorists would fly Potter back

138

here after the kidnapping. They could hold him so safely down there. Now it begins to make sense, don't you think, Mr. Styles? Potter was never in Carrados, never made the trip there."

"So we both arrive at the same conclusion, but where does it get us?" Peter said.

"You follow one trail for months and come up empty," Santos said. "Then you see a new trail. Maybe you come up not so empty." He sipped his drink. "Potter is an important political asset to the terrorists. The Mason girl, Marcia's friend, is, unfortunately, just a nuisance. If anything can still be done for her it better be done quickly."

"She doesn't know anything. I'd swear to that," Peter said.

"Maybe not," Santos said. "Maybe they thought she did—knowing her connection with Potter—when all the time she didn't. But she knows something now. She knows who took her, where she's been held. Her prospects are very poor, Mr. Styles."

"Try Peter," Peter said.

"Thank you—Peter."

"You're willing to help her?"

"We are used to violent death in my part of the world," Santos said. "Kidnappings and assassinations are a part of our everyday political life. Pick up the paper today—any day—and you will read about the kidnapping of politicians, the assassination of three or four rightists or leftists, depending on the climate. Terrorist attacks on whole groups of people we have every day for breakfast. The kidnapping of foreigners, diplomats or big business executives, is commonplace. There was the kidnapping of an executive of Owens-Illinois in Venezuela—just like the Potter case. We shrug off this kind of violence every day, Peter. I report the facts as I see them. I do not take sides. If the terrorists pass on their demands to me, I transmit them. If the rightists pass on their demands to me, I transmit. If I were to editorialize on the facts I get, take sides, I would be very quickly dead. The people in my world would read about it and

139

say, 'That's the way it is—*C'est la vie.*' "

"So you can't help us because you don't dare help us," Peter said.

"I did not say that, Peter. You, when you write your story, will take sides. I, when I print my story, will tell only facts and let the readers choose up sides. But Marcia's friend—?" The bright smile never left him. "Perhaps I can help, but it must not look as if I have helped."

"How can you help? And how can you help in a hurry?" Peter asked. "You've already said it, you know. Lynn Mason's prospects are poor."

"I know, I know, Peter. Sometimes help does not involve producing something positive. Sometimes just eliminating things is helpful. Marcia told you that I found her at Kennedy only a few minutes after you'd left. She told me what she knows —or thinks she knows—and about her friend, Lynn Mason. I am a skeptical man. I know my kind of people, the people from my world. We are a people with passionate causes and beliefs, Peter, but we are not plain damn fools. You understand?"

"Not yet," Peter said, impatience rising.

"I have contacts here in New York, just as I suppose you have contacts in other parts of the world," Santos said. "People who know the gossip. People who hear the talk. I asked questions, and the answers may surprise you."

"The questions also interest me," Peter said.

"But of course. The questions will tell you almost as much as the answers. Question number one: I ask if they have heard the rumor that Potter, after his kidnapping in Carrados, was brought back to this country. They had heard the rumor. They had heard Miss Mason's contention. They said they did not believe it for an instant. Why would the terrorists make it ten times harder for themselves—to hold Potter safely? Question number two: Did they believe it was possible Potter never went to Carrados, that he was kidnapped here? They did not believe

140

that either. Why risk a kidnapping here when it could be managed so easily in Carrados? The terrorists could have waited for Potter to go to Carrados if he was the man they wanted for some special reason. What would be the hurry? They have negotiated now for four months. They could have waited hours or days if necessary without running the risks of a violent action here. If they just wanted an important man, there are men even more important than Potter in Carrados. My friends think kidnapping him here made no sense."

"But it was done," Peter said. "If Marcia's right, it was done here."

"Yes, yes, of course," Santos said. He was like an excited child. "And then my friends asked me a question. Was Potter really kidnapped by the Carrados terrorists? Could someone else be responsible and have blamed it on the terrorists? Why the not-Potter passenger on Marcia's plane? If the kidnapping appeared to take place in Carrados, it would lend belief to the notion that the terrorists were responsible."

"But the terrorists have been negotiating for Potter's release for four months," Peter said.

"They would take advantage," Santos said. "How do you say it in poker? The hole card? If someone believes their hole card is Potter, they would bargain for anything, take advantage. You see? Even though their real hole card was the joker."

"One of their people was killed who brought answers from Potter to four questions that only Potter could answer. It doesn't hold water, Jaymie. Interesting, but as we say—no cigar."

"Exactly what I said to my friends," Santos said, still beaming, delighted with the game. "Their answer to me went something like this, Peter. It is no secret, they said to me, that there are people within the organization of Harkness Chemical who are jealous of the power of other people in that same organization. Those people conspire with the terrorists and if, in the end,

141

the Perrault government falls and the terrorists take power then those people within Harkness who have helped them will run an expropriated Harkness Chemical for the new people in power. The terrorists would need their know-how. The profits would be shared. My friends think that may be the way it is, and you and I have to take it seriously, Peter. Isn't this Colonel Keach high up in Harkness, and didn't he engineer the flight of the not-Potter man to Carrados? You have to begin to believe, don't you see? It all fits together too perfectly. It is what you would call a civil war at the top levels in Harkness Chemical. The terrorists take advantage and cooperate with one side. Potter is the sacrificial lamb. It is even rumored, among my friends, that Colonel Keach is involved with Potter's wife. So Potter is chosen to be the hostage so that in the end they can be rid of him."

"And Lynn Mason?" The whole idea was spinning around in Peter's head. It could be. It explained many things. It even helped to explain Gabriel Zorn who would have to be on one side or the other in a power struggle.

"I am not too happy about your Lynn Mason," Santos said. "Why would they burden themselves with another hostage? I'm afraid I think you should look for her in your city morgue, an unidentified accident victim."

Peter might have brushed aside Santos's story as a wild imagining if Walter Franklin, the State Department man, hadn't suggested a version of it. His suggestion had been that Harkness Chemical was allied with the terrorists, the kidnapping a public excuse for passing on working money to the terrorists. Santos's story was a variation; one group in Harkness Chemical trying to seize power from another group. Potter and Lynn Mason scapegoats in either case.

"There is one other thing," Marcia Lewis said. She looked huddled, small, frightened in the corner of the couch. "About Sam Evans and his not making the trip to Carrados with the man who was supposed to be Potter."

"They had to be sure he couldn't make the trip because they couldn't have kept him away from the supposed Potter. Potter was his friend and associate," Santos said. "It was announced that Evans had overslept and missed the plane. Evans, at some point, said he had been drugged at a party—how do you say it? —someone had 'slipped him a Mickey.'"

"That's the way the script reads," Peter said.

"My friends know where Evans was that night," Santos said. "It's a place people from my world frequent here in New York. It is called Mamma's International Club. Do you know it, Peter?"

Peter shook his head.

"Mamma Ortega is from Mexico," Santos said. "Her husband, Juan Ortega, was in politics—on the left. He died in the bombing of an airport some years ago—in Mexico. Mamma established a business for herself here in New York, and it is very popular, specially with Spanish-speaking people and the friends of Spanish-speaking people. A bar, a restaurant, and— how shall I put it?—a glorified massage parlor. Liquor, food, girls. It can be a very gay place."

"Jaymie's friends say that Sam spent the evening there, the night before the flight to Carrados," Marcia said.

"He passed out there," Santos said. "Mamma Ortega let him spend the night there."

"You're suggesting that someone at this International Club drugged him?" Peter asked.

Santos shrugged. "He passed out there," he said. "It might be worth while to ask a few questions. Who knows, Keach may have been there that night."

"You think Keach may have been a regular customer there?"

Marcia Lewis was looking down at her hands, tightly locked in her lap. "He took me there one night, some months ago," she said.

Peter glanced at his watch. "I am to make a call about Colonel Keach in a few minutes. Then maybe you will introduce me to Mamma Ortega. Change your mind about a drink, Marcia?"

"I think I will," she said.

Walter Franklin had come up with considerable material on Weldon Keach. As he gave it to him over the phone Peter took notes. Marcia and Jaymie Santos sat across the room, sipping drinks, hearing only Peter's end of the conversation, which revealed nothing.

Born in Great Barrington, Massachusetts—small town. Only child of Harry and Mathilda Keach. Harry Keach, an independent insurance agent, prosperous, still alive and kicking.... Local grade and high school, Williams College in Williamstown, Mass., Alpha Chi Rho fraternity, football, winter sports. R.O.T.C.... Harvard Business School for two years and then enlisted in the Air Force, R.O.T.C. starting him off with the rank of lieutenant. Served in Vietnam with a brilliant record as a bomber pilot.

"Of some interest to you," Franklin interjected. "His copilot during a two-year stretch was one Wilfred Hadley. Hadley, a few years older, had gone into service from his job as a junior executive at Harkness Chemical. This connection brought Keach into Harkness after they were out of service. Keach had risen to the rank of colonel, Hadley a captain. Both military records spotless."

The notes went on.

Hadley's father in diplomatic service, now dead. His mother a Venezuelan. Hadley spoke fluent Spanish which landed him a job in Carrados....

"I give you Hadley because the tie-in with Keach seems so close," Franklin said.

Keach at first did odd jobs for Harkness, among them flying the company's private jets. This took him to Harkness interests all over the world. It may be significant, it may be accidental, but he often piloted Potter, a sort of diplomatic trouble shooter for the corporation. They became friends outside of business. Keach often a guest at the Potters' home. . . . It is suggested that Potter or Potter's wife called Keach to the attention of Robert Harkness, with the result that Keach seems to have climbed more rapidly in the Harkness hierarchy than might have been expected. . . . Trusted with secret missions, sometimes with Potter, sometimes on his own. Not possible to report on the nature of these missions, but he touched down often at Carrados where he and Hadley were, not unnaturally, seen together. . . . Personal habits: He drinks, but alcohol not a problem. Womanizer in spades. One in every port. His name linked with Frances Potter. Rumor has it that Mrs. Potter isn't a one-man woman by any means. Keach takes care of himself physically, squash in cold climate winters, golf and tennis in warm weather. . . . He is said to be a man of violent temper. Barroom brawls not unusual. It doesn't show anywhere, but it is rumored that Harkness Chemical paid off out of court a whopping damage suit brought against Keach for "assault and battery" on a South American businessman visiting in New York at a place called Mamma's International Club. This is important, perhaps, because it indicates how much Harkness Chemical thinks of Keach. The damage suit is said to have run into a healthy six figures.

145

"That's it for now," Franklin said on the phone.

"I was just headed for this International Club to ask questions about Keach," Peter said.

Franklin chuckled. "I imagine Mamma Ortega will have plenty to say about him. She was damn near put out of business as a result of that brawl. Enough big shots are customers of hers to have saved her hide. I'm naturally curious about your interest in Keach."

"Like you say," Peter said, " 'it is rumored' that he may have had something to do with Potter's kidnapping."

"So my theory had some meat on its bones? Harkness Chemical is playing along with the terrorists?"

"Maybe," Peter said. "Maybe just a faction in Harkness. Would the idea of a power struggle make any sense to you?"

"The old bull against the young bulls?" Franklin hesitated. "The time comes, doesn't it, when the old men fight to hang on and the young men grab for power."

"Keach, Hadley and company against Robert Harkness?"

"If that's the way it is I'd guess the Old Man could still handle those two with one hand tied behind him."

"If they hit him in a weak spot—through his son-in-law?"

"The Old Man might deal for a while," Franklin said, "but my guess is he wouldn't throw in the towel to save anyone."

"Not even Potter?"

"Not even his own child is my guess—if it came down to that." Franklin sounded almost as if he felt an admiration for Robert Harkness. "You don't build yourself an empire with the word 'surrender' in your vocabulary."

"I'm grateful for your help, Mr. Franklin."

"Keep in touch, if you can," Franklin said. "You've got my curiosity into high gear."

Peter rejoined Marcia and Santos. They tried to look uncurious but there had been too many names mentioned on Peter's

146

end of the conversation.

"A dossier on Keach," Peter said, folding his notes and slipping them into an inside pocket. "One of the more interesting bits is that he and Wilfred Hadley flew together in Vietnam, are old friends."

"I could have told you that," Santos said. "It's common knowledge in Carrados. In his leisure time Hadley talked endlessly about his war experiences—and they included his friend Keach."

"I think perhaps we'd better go talk to Mamma Ortega," Peter said.

"There is one thing, Peter," Marcia said. "You haven't shown Jaymie that drawing of a man you showed me at the hangar."

Peter crossed to his desk and took the police-artist's drawing out of the manila envelope. He handed it to Santos, who sat scowling at it for a moment. Then Santos slapped the drawing with the back of his hand and looked up at Peter with that bright smile.

"I know this man!" he said. "That is to say, I know who he is. An actor."

Peter shook his head. "The Harkness computer came up with that," he said. "Paul Newman is alive and well and working in England."

"No, no, not Paul Newman," Santos said. "A Latin American. Juan Fernandez I think it is. He makes many Spanish-language films, commercials for the television. He spends, I think, a good part of his time in this country dubbing in the Spanish language for television shows and films to be exported to South America. Kojak speaks Spanish in South America, you know? I don't know if Fernandez speaks for Kojak, but he speaks for many other actors. Why do you have this picture?"

Peter explained. "The man is not expected to pull through," he concluded. "I'm naturally interested because he was asking

147

for me. Shall we go?"

Mamma's International Club was not like any place Peter had ever seen before. You didn't just walk in off the street. You had to meet with the approval of some sort of gateman who peered at you through an iron grill in a heavy oak door. The house the door protected was an old-fashioned brownstone in the Murray Hill district. It must have been the height of elegance in Stanford White's day. They had no trouble with the gateman. Santos was given a hearty greeting and his guests were welcome.

The ground floor of the house had been extensively remodeled from the living room-dining room-library-kitchen of a private home. Partitions had been knocked out to make one huge room of it, a long mahogany bar covering one wall. There were elegant Victorian tables and chairs and one or two love seats, all upholstered in a wine-colored material. The murals on the walls were somewhat startling; lovely naked ladies painted in the style of the Renaissance. Little animals cavorted admiringly around the ladies—little lambs, little dogs, a sly fox peering from behind a painted shrubbery.

At the bar there were a dozen live girls, almost naked, Peter observed. There were perhaps only eight or ten customers at the moment, each attended by one of the ladies of the house. The ladies viewed Marcia with some hostility. Outside competition cut into the trade.

It was only about seven o'clock as they walked up to the bar and Santos asked to see Mamma Ortega. While they waited he explained that the place would be crowded later in the evening. He laughed. "Mamma Ortega may not yet have had her breakfast," he said. "The last customers do not leave till daylight."

Word came that Mamma would receive them in her private office at the rear, and they were led there by a waiter.

Mamma Ortega was something to behold. She had red hair, a color red that Nature never dreamed of. She was made up like a glamor queen of the 1920s. Her face was wrinkled but somehow youthful in its expression. She still had an elegant figure, though she must be in her sixties. She received them in a lavender housecoat that fell to the floor, revealing only the tips of silver slippers. She was smoking a cigarette in a long ivory holder, and she held a brandy glass in her left hand, half full.

She greeted Santos effusively. "Jaymie, love, it has been too long!" She held out her arms, cigarette in one hand, drink in the other. Santos embraced her and kissed her, rather lingeringly, on the mouth. "Oh, it has been too long, and you came too late in the first place. If I'd had you forty years ago, young man, I'd have—well, never mind what I would have done to you." The voice was hoarse, long ago wrecked by cigarettes and liquor. She turned with a polite, inquiring smile to Peter and Marcia. Then she gave a cackle of delight. "I know this young lady!" she said. "I once offered her permanent employment when she came here with the kind of man who should be forced to pay for his pleasures instead of getting them free. Have you changed your mind, young woman?"

"I'm afraid not, Mamma," Marcia said. "I asked Jaymie to bring me and my friend Mr. Styles because Mr. Styles is interested in that man you referred to."

Mamma's face darkened. "Keach? That animal!" She glared at Peter. "If you have come here for a character reference, you won't get it, young man."

"I've come to find out all I can about him, and also about a particular night here," Peter said. "Let me say I am not Keach's friend."

"You want to know about the night Keach turned my club into a boxing arena?" Mamma asked.

"I hope you'll tell us," Peter said. "But the night I am interested in was four months and fifteen days ago, March the third. It was the night when Sam Evans passed out and spent the night here."

149

"Oh my God!" Mamma said. Then her eyes narrowed. "It has just been on the seven o'clock news. I was watching it when they told me you were here. Sam has been murdered! Are you from the police, Styles?"

"Mamma, would I bring a policeman to your club?" Santos asked.

"Peter is a friend of a friend of Sam's who is in great trouble," Marcia said. "He thinks Weldon Keach maybe responsible for that trouble. And that friend of Sam's is also a friend of mine."

"I know you, Styles!" Mamma said, pointing a finger at him. "You are a newspaper reporter!"

"But not here to get a story from you as a reporter, Mamma Ortega," Peter said. "I need help in order to help a friend. That friend may be murdered by the same people who murdered Sam Evans if I can't prevent it."

"Fill my glass, Jaymie," Mamma said, handing it to Santos. "Make something for yourself and your friends if you like."

The room wasn't large. The walls were hung with heavy lavender drapes, a darker shade of lavender than the lady's housecoat. There were no windows, but there was, obviously, noiseless air conditioning. The flat-top desk, the heavy, carved chairs were out of another century. The lighting was indirect.

Santos bought the henna-haired Mamma a full glass of brandy, got a "no thanks" signal from Peter and Marcia.

"Which do you want first, Styles?" Mamma Ortega asked. "Poor dear little Sammy, or that monster, Keach?"

"Sammy first, if you will," Peter said. "The one may lead to the other."

Mamma sat down on the edge of her desk, and in that position the split down the front of her housecoat revealed an expanse of leg that would have made many younger women happy.

"There is not much to tell you, Styles," she said. "About Sammy's night. It started like many nights, because he came

150

here many nights. Poor Sammy, he was in love and the lady he loved had walked off with someone else."

Lynn Mason had walked off with Richard Potter, Peter knew.

"Much of my clients are Latin American," Mamma said. "I am myself from Mexico, but I have lived here so long I sound like from Brooklyn or the Bronx. No?"

"You sound like Mamma Ortega, no more, no less," Santos said. He had a way with this woman.

"Well, Sammy, when his lady left him, started to come here often. He came first with someone from Carrados where he had been. He spoke a little Spanish. He was charming, but he was not interested in the girls. While his friend went upstairs for a little dalliance, he talked to me. I am Mamma, no? So he told me about his broken heart. The next time, or the time after that, he will be interested in one of the girls, I told myself. But he wasn't. But he enjoyed himself. Maybe the third or fourth time he said to me that he was not interested in the specialty of the house—that was the way he put it—and that if that made him not welcome I should say so. He enjoyed my company, he said, he liked to laugh, he liked to slap a round little behind now and then—but that was all. Well, there is a profit at the bar. Not so good a profit as there is with the girls, but a profit. So I told him—welcome!"

"The night he passed out, Mamma. The night of March third," Peter said, trying not to show his impatience.

"As I said, it was like any other night. He came!" She shrugged. " 'I won't see you for a few days, Mamma,' he said to me. 'Going on a trip. Be sure and get me out of here by eleven o'clock. We take off at twelve-thirty.' He went to the bar. He laughed and joked with some of the girls there. They had come to like him. It fascinated them that none of them could interest him. He wasn't homosexual, you know? A woman can tell. I was not paying any attention, you understand? There were

151

other customers. It was just a little after ten o'clock when Sammy fell off his bar stool and lay flat on his face on the floor. He had passed out—how you say, cold?"

"Early in the evening, wasn't it?" Peter asked.

"*Si*—yes, very early. And nothing like this had ever happened before. He was a very good man with liquor, never out of line. He had been at the bar for about an hour and a half. He had had three double bourbons—about average for him for that time. The bartender was keeping a tab for him, you see. He didn't pay with each drink. Well, he must have had a great deal to drink before he came in, I thought, though I hadn't noticed. We carried him back here to my apartment. We tried to bring him to enough to get some hot coffee into him. We tried everything we knew because he said he must leave at eleven—for his trip. But nothing would revive him. You know, I am an old hand at this sort of thing and I was worried. So there is a nice doctor who lives a couple of blocks away who sometimes enjoys the company of my girls. He doesn't make house calls, but he came. A man like that, in his position, does not say no to Mamma Ortega."

Benevolent blackmail, Peter thought.

"So the doctor tried this and that and then he asked me, 'Did you slip him a Mickey, Mamma?' Well, of course no one slipped him a Mickey, not in the Club International. If I lost the trust of my patrons I would lose my business. But the doctor could not bring him to. He said just to let Sammy sleep it out. He would call back in the morning. So there was no way I could get Sammy off to his trip. In time he woke up—the next morning. He was bewildered. I told him everything, how we had called a doctor, how we had done everything we could. You know what he said? He said, 'Someone must have slipped me a Mickey!' But he didn't mean it. Not that time. Later—?" She shrugged.

"He suggested it again later?" Peter asked.

"You know about the trip he missed, Styles? Everybody knows. The trip was to Carrados with Richard Potter. Richard Potter was kidnapped by the terrorists. Everybody knows that. Richard Potter was Sammy's boss. Sammy thought if he hadn't missed the trip he might have prevented the kidnapping. I told him that was nonsense. I told him that two men against an army of terrorists is not better than one man against an army of terrorists. And he said, 'Somebody slipped me a Mickey, Mamma, so that I couldn't make the trip.' And this time he meant it. 'Well, no one slipped you a Mickey here,' I told him. 'Eduardo, my bartender, has been with me for twenty-eight years. Would he slip you a Mickey?' Sammy said he didn't suspect Eduardo. 'Do you think I would countenance anyone slipping you a Mickey?' I asked him. He said he knew I would not. 'So if anyone slipped you a Mickey it happened before you came here,' I told him. 'It worked here, but you didn't get it here.' And do you know what he told me, Styles? He told me that he hadn't had a drink anywhere that night until he came here. He came back once or twice after that, but since then I haven't seen him."

"Did he suggest who might have drugged him?" Peter asked.
"He trusted you and Eduardo."

Mamma spread her jeweled wrists and hands. "One of the girls, he thought. Why, because he wouldn't go upstairs with them? The girls liked him. They wouldn't do him harm just because he chose not to be a customer."

"And yet, one of the girls may have drugged him," Peter said. "She couldn't have had a motive you haven't thought of, Mamma?"

"What motive? What possible kind of motive?" Mamma sounded outraged.

"A favor for a friend," Peter said. "Let's go to the second one, Colonel Weldon Keach."

"Gross pig!" Mamma said.

153

"A handsome man. I've seen him, Mamma."

"Handsome is as handsome does," Mamma said. "I know him well. He was a regular customer—three, four nights a week. At first I thought he was very gay, very much fun, full of laughter and juices. But then I began to hear complaints from the girls. This one enjoys cruelty, fancy ways of inflicting pain. Most of the girls wanted no further dealings with him."

"Most?" Peter asked.

"There are a couple of my regular girls who will do anything, subject themselves to anything, for an extra fee."

"We will come to them," Peter said. "But first, let me ask you to remember. Was Weldon Keach here the night Sammy Evans passed out?"

"*Por Dios*—no!" Mamma almost shouted. "That night was *after* my trouble with the animal Keach! I remember the date very well, because lawyers, and policemen, and the security person for Harkness Chemical—they all ask questions over and over."

"Gabriel Zorn?"

Mamma Ortega's eyes brightened. "A very droll fellow," she said. "He was, he said, too old for the kind of pleasures we offer here. When you are too old is just the time for it, I told him. He just laughed. But the date you ask for was January twenty-eighth, more than a month before the night Sammy passed out. Keach was never admitted to my place again after nearly killing a man with his fists in front of my customers. What has he got to do with Sammy?"

"He was the pilot of the plane Sammy missed that night."

"But of course! They both work for Harkness Chemical, no?"

"And the real reason I am here, Mamma, is because I believe Keach didn't want Sam Evans to take that trip to Carrados. So I think Keach may have been responsible for the drugged drink that knocked Sam Evans out."

"But Keach was not here, I promise you that."

"How about the one or two girls who didn't object to pleasing him for an extra fee? Were those girls present the night Sam Evans passed out? A favor for a friend, I said, Mamma. It could also be a favor for a fee."

The bright, mascaraed eyes glittered. "That bitch!" she said. "Yes, Styles, there is one who might sell me out—might sell out her own mother—for a fee. She is one who accepted Keach as a customer. I would have sent her packing long ago, but several of my best customers—" Mamma shrugged. "The customer is always right, no?"

It was early in the evening for the main traffic to have begun at the International Club. It turned out that Vicki Taylor's first customer had not yet arrived. Miss Taylor was a well-stacked blonde who sauntered into Mamma's office, obviously thinking some new customer had asked for her. Mamma quickly disabused her of that idea.

"Mr. Styles, here, needs to know the truth about something, Vicki," she said. "Tell him the truth and I will only loathe you a little more than I already do. Lie to him and I will have you thrown into the next garbage-crushing machine that comes to collect."

Apparently outbursts from Mamma were not unusual, but the blonde girl looked warily at Peter. He could see that she suspected cop.

"Have you watched the seven o'clock news on television, Vicki?" Peter asked.

"As a matter of fact I did," she said.

"So you know that Sam Evans was murdered," Peter said.

"How do you like that? He used to be a good customer here."

"Until after the night you put knockout drops in his drink at the bar," Peter said, in a conversational tone.

It obviously threw her off balance. "What the hell are you talking about, man?"

"Now you are at the moment of big decision," Mamma

155

Ortega said. "You tell the truth and I forgive you, even though I may choke on it. Lie, stall around, play games, and I will make you wish you had never been born, Vicki."

"Let me tell you, Vicki," Peter said, "That two lives may hang in the balance. Two people may be murdered by the same people who took care of Sam Evans. I think Weldon Keach persuaded you to slip Sam Evans a Mickey. What was it supposed to be? Some kind of joke? Keach told you Evans had a date with someone and he didn't want him to keep it?"

The girl had to make a quick choice and she did. "It was a joke," she said. "They were both interested in some girl—on the outside. There didn't seem to be any harm in it."

"Keach wasn't there that night. How did he get the word to you?"

"He—he called me on the telephone," Vicki said. She sounded rattled.

"And how did you get the drug you put into Sam Evans' drink?"

"I—I had it."

"You stupid bitch! I told you what would happen if you lied!" Mamma Ortega shouted at her. She turned to Peter. "She was seeing Keach on the outside, of course, which is against our rules. Giving a customer free on the outside what he has to pay for here on the inside is forbidden. It's bad business."

"Mamma!" the girl said unsteadily. "Mamma, I was afraid to refuse him. He is a dangerous man."

"And you were afraid to refuse when he gave you something to put into Sam Evans's drink?" Peter asked.

"If you knew this man, Mr. Styles!"

"I am beginning to know him," Peter said.

2

A whole segment of the puzzle had fallen into place. Peter might have wondered about the help from Gabriel Zorn that had taken him to Marcia at Kennedy. He might have questioned his own instincts about Marcia, even the sincerity of Jaymie Santos, but there was no way the fabulous Mamma Ortega or the frightened Vicki Taylor could have been acting.

So Peter now had a picture of the complex, perhaps psychotic, Weldon Keach, in on the kidnapping of Richard Potter from the start. In on the kidnapping and skillfully handling the charade with the phoney Potter so that he would have innocent witnesses to the fact that Potter had been seized in Carrados. Only one thing he couldn't have known, hadn't known, obviously, was that Marcia Lewis carried love notes between Potter and Lynn Mason. Everything else had been airtight. There had been two dangerous areas. The first was that Sam Evans might make too much noise about his having been drugged to keep him from making the trip. People being people, the feeling was that Sam was trying to cover up a drunken lapse. The second danger came when Sam Evans persuaded Lynn Mason to devise a question for Potter—a question only Potter could answer. "I was concerned about us" meant to Lynn that Potter was in the United States. No one else had taken that very seriously because it made no sense that the terrorists would fly Potter back to this country to hold him. Now it made complete sense. Potter had never left this country. The kidnapping had been managed here, not in Carrados. That much could be considered fact, and Keach's involvement in it could be considered fact.

Santos had suggested a power struggle within Harkness Chemical. It was a rumor he had picked up along his own private grapevine. It was the kind of rumor that must almost always be fact inside any big corporate structure. Peter thought he had seen the outlines of it on the penthouse of the Harkness Chemical Building that morning. The old bull and the young bull—Robert Harkness and Calvin Trevor. Harkness, standing by the old way of doing things that had made Harkness what it was, fighting to keep his hands on the controls; Calvin Trevor, seeing a changing times, even the need to change allegiances in Latin America from a conservative-oriented democracy to a left-oriented socialist regime. It became a judgment on which way the most products could be sold, the most profits made. Publicly you had to be cautious of your image, privately you went after the dollar. That was where men of different generations like Harkness and Trevor could split. It would be no problem, Peter thought, for Trevor to enlist the support of young soldiers of fortune in the organization like Keach and Wilfred Hadley. Keach works his way into the enemy stronghold through Frances Potter, the Old Man's daughter, who was obviously a sophisticated tramp. They strike at the Old Man by using his own son-in-law as a hostage. Hadley manages the transfer of ransom money from Harkness Chemical to the conspiracy.

But there was no time for speculation. How could he use what he now knew about Keach to help Lynn Mason? The sand in the glass must be running out for Lynn.

The problem was that what he now knew about Keach was

not evidence. What Peter knew for certain was that someone other than Potter had been flown out of the country by Keach. The fake Potter must have used Potter's travel permits, passport, and any other necessary documents. That was a crime, a crime committed by the fake Potter and by Keach as an accomplice. But how to prove it? Where was the fake Potter? Where was the proof that there had been a fake Potter? Keach would of course deny the whole thing and all they had was Marcia Lewis's certainty that the real Potter would not have refused to speak to her on the plane. Point to the careful maneuvering of Connors and Marcia by Keach so that it seemed quite natural they hadn't seen their passenger, and it still wouldn't hold up. Potter could have been the passenger and not seeing him could have been a curious, unpremeditated set of circumstances. Call in the Immigration Service, the CIA, the FBI, and if they tried to move on the evidence, no matter what they believed, all that would happen was that Keach would be alerted to their suspicions, his accomplices in the conspiracy would be alerted, and the cover-up would be made complete and total. The loose ends, like hostages, might be disposed of, and Keach, the only solid suspect they had, would laugh his way home from any interrogation.

Peter, Marcia Lewis, and Jaymie Santos sat in a corner booth at the rear of a little Third Avenue bar frequented by newspaper people in the area. Santos appeared to Peter like his best source of help, Santos with his Latin American connections and their rumors.

Santos wasn't hopeful. "My friends laughed at the idea that Potter had been flown back here from Carrados," he said. "No one suggested that Potter may never have left this country, so that wasn't a rumor they had heard. That means they have heard nothing about where Potter might be held here. If Potter and your Miss Mason were being held here by Latin American terrorists, I swear someone would have lowered an eyelid or smiled a smile that would have told me that. Keach, we know, is a party to the kidnapping, so I have to believe that the people who actually abducted Potter are not Latin Americans but good Anglo-Saxon members of one power group inside Harkness Chemical. So Potter could be in any one of a million apartments here in New York City. Your Miss Mason, too. Or even some suburban house or big estate. I don't think my sources have that information. So I don't think I can help you more than I have, Peter. In the sense of providing you with new facts. But I'm willing to help, of course. It is a big story for any reporter."

"The only lead we have is Keach," Peter said, a bitter note in his voice. "We can watch him and see where he takes us. It will probably be only to the Harkness Chemical Building where his friends and allies are. We can't follow him past the front door there."

"Without the help of your friend Zorn," Santos said.

"Is he my friend? That's the question there. He sent me to Marcia, she has brought me to Keach. Is that what he wanted? If there is a power struggle going on at Harkness, then Gabriel Zorn must be on somebody's side. Which side? Did he expect me to find out something that would hang Keach—and tell him about it? Or was he making sure Keach hadn't slipped up anywhere and, if he had, cover up for him. I could tell him what I know and he might help us find Lynn and Potter, or he might make it dead sure that we never find either one of them. I don't dare take a chance on him."

"So there is nothing left except to cover Keach—and pray," Santos said.

And more time would slide by, more relentless, irretrievable time. But what else? Peter called his trusted friends, Devery, Maxvil, and Walter Franklin, the State Department man. Each of them could help. Devery could assign another reporter to the story. Peter couldn't watch around the clock. Maxvil could

160

establish the fact of a crime if the man Keach had flown to Carrados on the third of March wasn't Potter. Franklin could dig, through his sources, to find out who was on what side in the power struggle at Harkness Chemical—if there was such a struggle. Most important, who did Gabriel Zorn belong to? Whose man was he? His age and the importance of his position would normally have suggested that he had come up with the old leadership of Robert Harkness. But Peter remembered Maxvil's mentioning casually that Zorn had come over to Harkness Chemical from the CIA about five years ago. Who had brought him over? Where did his loyalties lie?

The beginning point in the surveillance of Keach had to be at Richard Potter's apartment where Keach was admittedly staying to "protect" a grieving Frances Potter.

A few minutes before midnight that night, Keach drove up to the apartment building in a taxi and went in. The chances were a hundred to one that he wouldn't come out again that night. It was agreed that Peter would meet Santos there early the next morning, along with the reporter Devery would assign, so they could all identify Keach when he came out and then split up the assignment.

More hours ticked away. In the early dawn Peter, catnapping in his apartment, had two reports. Maxvil had it from official sources that Richard Potter had made the flight to Carrados in Harkness Chemical's private jet. So a crime had been committed if you could prove that Potter's identity had been used by someone else.

"Incidentally, Greg, I forgot to tell you I found out who the man in Bellevue is," Peter said.

"Nice of you to remember now," Maxvil said. "Who is he?"

"A Latin American actor, apparently well known down there, named Juan Fernandez. He does work here dubbing Spanish-language dialogue into TV shows and films. He may actually have a pad somewhere here in New York."

161

"Better late than never," Maxvil said sourly, and hung up.

And then, just as Peter was dozing off again, Walter Franklin called.

"You are going to owe me the best and longest-eating dinner in town," he told Peter. "Your questions are driving me up the wall because I don't know why you're asking them. Sooner or later you're going to have to pay with answers. However—"

The essence of what Franklin had was what they had guessed at in the first place. Robert Harkness, after hanging on for forty years as founder, policy maker, boss of Harkness Chemical, was coming to the end of the line. Seventy-one years old, Harkness, if he had been anyone else, would have been retired by now on a handsome pension. But Robert Harkness was special and he would probably go on fighting as long as he could to hang onto some vestiges of control.

"The natural successor, you might say the heir apparent," Franklin said, "is Calvin Trevor. Over the years he has been Harkness's most trusted lieutenant. But this isn't just a little office squabble, you understand, Styles—who will be the next sales manager. Latin America is only a part of the picture. There are Harkness complexes in Europe, the Middle East, and Pentagon affiliations here in the United States. Each one of those complexes is headed by a man you have to believe would like to become the top boss."

"Who decides when the time comes?" Peter asked.

"A board of directors, which includes all these key people plus some heavy stockholders. Calvin Trevor is the Latin American expert. It could be that his position is a little shaky because of the Potter kidnapping and the paying of a hell of a lot in ransom that hasn't produced results. The Middle East man's name is Emile Varoody. The European man is Carl Forman. The Pentagon guy is Lou Bragan. So far they're just names to me, Styles. But the struggle may lie between one of them and Trevor. Or something else. The Old Man will have to quit sometime. He is the biggest single stockholder in the corporation. He probably has enough friends on the board of directors to swing a decision. While I sit here losing sleep I have asked myself a question."

"Are you going to hold out on me?" Peter asked.

"No, although I ought to. The kidnapping of Potter, his son-in-law, could bring a special kind of pressure on Robert Harkness. Someone is demanding his vote and the votes of his friends at decision time."

"Being asked to vote for a successor he wouldn't normally choose?" Peter asked.

"Perhaps that and his own immediate resignation—so that the transfer of power would become total right now."

"People keep telling me Harkness would sell out his own daughter if it was a choice between her and power," Peter said.

"Maybe—long ago," Franklin said. "But Robert Harkness can't defeat age; he can't stop growing old. This year, next year he has to give up with or without a struggle. He's just being hurried a little. It's just a notion, Styles. Right now I can't give you any kind of educated guess as to who's applying the pressure."

"I can tell you this much," Peter said. "Someone very close to the Old Man has sold him out."

"From your earlier questions I'm guessing Keach."

"Right on," Peter said. "And from what I've seen that means his own daughter, too. What about Gabriel Zorn? Anything on him?"

"You're a fascinating fellow, Styles," Franklin said. "I'll have to remember not to let you in my front door if you're after a story on me. Always get your man?"

"I wish I could say so," Peter said. "Right now I'm not very close to saving the lives of two people who have no one else looking out for them. Gabriel Zorn just might be on the right side of this fight. That's why I need to know about him."

"Sorry for the comedy," Franklin said. "Zorn was in the CIA for twenty years. Good record there. You can't get any kind of a detailed rundown on former agents. Matter of security. Some crackpot from an area where a man has been involved might take it into his head to do a violence. But Zorn had high marks, wherever he worked. What I think interests you is the fact that Calvin Trevor went shopping for a man and came up with Zorn."

"So he's Trevor's man," Peter said.

"Not necessarily. It would have been Trevor's job, as executive vice-president in charge of operations, to fill such an important post as chief of security. But I have no way of knowing who may have recommended Zorn to Trevor—or if there was any contact between Zorn and Trevor before the hiring—or Zorn and anyone else in the corporation. I don't think the fact that Trevor hired him has to mean he's Trevor's man. I'll keep working on it if it's iimportant."

"It is important," Peter said. "If there was someone in the corporation I could trust—Zorn has tried to make me think he might be believable, but it could be he just hopes I'll buy that idea and pass on information to him, let him keep one step ahead of me all the way."

"Do what I can," Franklin said.

And so another day came around, and Lynn Mason had been missing for thirty-six hours. They could have moved her to Alaska by now. Shortly before seven o'clock Peter was on the corner across the street from the Potters' apartment building with Jaymie Santos and a young man from Devery's staff named Bill Duncan. Duncan was an eager type, with a hero-worshipping attitude toward Peter. Working on a story with Peter was a special excitement for him.

"It's going to be a tedious business," Peter warned his two aides. "Keach may walk out of that building, take a taxi to the

Harkness Building, and spend the day at the office. That's the most likely thing."

"What about Kennedy? The Harkness planes are out there." Santos spread his hands in a Latin gesture. "He takes to the air and flies to God knows where."

"Marcia is going to keep us covered out there if she can," Peter said.

"What do you hope Keach does?" Bill Duncan asked.

"Good question. We hope he may meet with someone who would point to someone inside the office, or to the Harkness operation in Carrados, or to the terrorist organization. Santos might help us there. Ideally, we hope he leads us to where they are holding Potter and Lynn Mason."

Santos reached out and grabbed Peter's arm. "Jesus, Peter! Look across the street! You see that woman coming out of the apartment building? The one in the black dress with the little white hat?"

"I see her," Peter said.

"Now that is something hot!" Santos said. "That woman is Lupe Vargas, one of the top people in the terrorist movement in Carrados. She is maybe number three most important in leadership. And here she is, walking right out of the building where Keach is."

"The last time I saw her," Peter said, "she was called Juliana and she was Frances Potter's maid."

Santos was wide-eyed, his perpetual grin missing. "But if that is so, Keach is in with the very top people! My friends who hear things have either been very close mouthed with me, or Lupe Vargas's presence here is a very big secret even from the people who hear secrets! This Vargas woman, she blows up bridges, she is an assassin, she fights in the front lines with the men soldiers. She is a very tough woman, Peter!"

Lupe Vargas walking down the avenue in the bright morning

sunlight looked like a plump, middle-aged housewife. She would have attracted no more attention than a thousand other Spanish-speaking housewives in the Puerto Rican sections of the city. Her masquerade as Frances Potter's maid seemed to lock up the theory that at least one faction in Harkness Chemical was selling out to the terrorists.

"Let me follow her, Peter," Santos said. "You are interested in a headquarters—a terrorist headquarters. She could lead us there."

"Go," Peter said.

He and Bill Duncan watched Jaymie move out and head quickly down the avenue on the opposite side of the street from the Vargas woman.

Five minutes later Keach, his summer straw hat raked over one eye at a jaunty Clark Gable angle, emerged from the apartment house across the way, signaling for a taxi.

"Go with him, Bill," Peter said to Duncan. "He may just take you to the Harkness Building. Try me at this number if he lights somewhere." Peter had scribbled the pay phone number on a slip of paper.

"Do my best," Duncan said.

The young man got a break. There was a second cab cruising down the avenue behind the one that Keach flagged.

Peter stood alone in the corner of the little shop, having assuaged the shopkeeper's curiosity with his press card and a five spot. He was thinking about the luscious Frances Potter, wife of the kidnapped man, daughter of the old bull, Robert Harkness, lover of the man who had arranged a fake kidnapping, who had staged the drugging of Sam Evans, perhaps even his eventual murder. Where did this complex woman's loyalties really lie? Certainly not with her husband. Was she Keach's all the way, working with him for some kind of deal with the terrorists, a deal which would finish her father? Peter had heard it said so often that the Old Man would sell out anyone if his power was threatened—his own daughter if it came down to that. Like father, like daughter? Did this glamorous woman, brought up in a climate of power, see world power for herself if she threw in with Keach against her husband and her father? Keach and Hadley and God knows what other young bulls at Harkness Chemical, headed by a Harkness, dealing with a top woman leader in the terrorist movement? It could be a dangerous combination.

The pay phone rang and Peter, glancing at his watch, realized his friends had been gone for a good twenty minutes. It was Bill Duncan on the phone.

"Our man has apparently gone to visit someone at Bellevue Hospital," Duncan said. "I'm in the reception lobby there now. Keach is talking to someone at the desk."

"Listen to me, Bill," Peter said, his voice tense. "Listen to me like you've never listened. There is a patient there in intensive care. He may have a name, Juan Fernandez. The hospital may not know his name yet, but he was brought in day before yesterday from the Hotel Beaumont, victim of an attempted homicide. Don't let Keach get to him, Bill."

"How do I stop him?"

"I don't know, Bill. Throw a fit, scream for help, call for the police and bring charges, but don't let Keach get to Fernandez. Fernandez may have answers that Keach can't afford to let him give to anyone."

"Suppose Keach is just here to visit his maiden aunt from Des Moines?"

"Not a chance in the world, boy. There aren't any coincidences like that. I'll try to get help as quickly as I can, but don't let Keach out of your sight or anywhere near Fernandez."

"Do my best," Duncan said, and the phone went dead.

Peter tried Maxvil again. Damn Maxvil. Why would he choose this moment to be unreachable? The desk officer in

Maxvil's office sounded impatient. This was the third time Peter had called.

"Look, Mr. Styles, I promise the lieutenant will get the message to call you the minute he checks in."

"I won't be where he can reach me," Peter said. "Just tell him Weldon Keach is at Bellevue Hospital looking for Fernandez. That will get him off his butt."

Peter stood staring across the street at the apartment building. Frances Potter was without two of her allies at the moment, Keach at Bellevue, Lupe Vargas headed somewhere with Santos on her trail. She could very well be alone in the apartment.

He looked in the Manhattan telephone directory and found Richard Potter's number. He dialed it with fingers that weren't quite steady. After about three rings the unmistakably rich voice of Frances Potter came on the line.

"Yes."

"Mrs. Potter?" This is Peter Styles. I—"

"Now look, Mr. Styles, I will not be annoyed by you and your questions. There is nothing I know that can be of any use to you or your story."

"I have called to warn you," Peter said.

"Warn me?"

"If Keach isn't stopped from getting to Juan Fernandez in the hospital you will find yourself being charged with being an accomplice in a homicide. Out of that will come kidnapping charges. You have just about one chance of spending the rest of your life out of jail. Tell me the truth, and help me to stop Keach."

There was a moment's pause. The accomplished actress was at work again. "Where are you, Mr. Styles?"

"Directly across the street from your building."

"What you're saying doesn't make the slightest sense, but I'm willing to show you how absurd you're being. The doorman will have instructions to let you up."

168

3

Afterward Peter realized he should have recognized it was too long a shot, and that Frances Potter fell for it just a little too easily. He told himself he had enough, without waiting for legal reinforcements, to make Frances Potter see that the game was played out, that releasing Lynn and Richard Potter unharmed could reduce the severity of the punishment she faced. If Keach made a move toward Fernandez in the hospital, they had him cold, without having to prove the details of the phoney flight to Carrados or the drugging of Sam Evans. The presence of Lupe Vargas, masquerading as a maid, was all that was needed to show her and Keach's link to the terrorists. It was more than enough for a showdown, Peter thought. The closer they came to some kind of legal proof, the less chance there was that Lynn and Richard Potter would ever be set free, able to talk. Frances Potter, her father's daughter, could probably be a very tough cookie, but she was almost certainly a realist. She would see that she and her partners were only a step or two away from destruction. That's the way Peter saw it as he crossed the avenue and walked into the lobby of the apartment house.

The doorman, hostile on his first visit, gave him a professional smile.

169

"Mrs. Potter says you are to go straight up, Mr. Styles," he said. "Fourteen B."

The man at the house switchboard gestured toward the elevator. The welcome mat was spread out.

He took the noiseless self-service elevator to Fourteen and rang the doorbell of Apartment B. Frances Potter opened the door almost at once. This woman, he thought, could look marvelous pretty early in the morning. She was wearing a black linen suit and a little straw hat with flowers. A handbag and a pair of white gloves were on a table beside the front door.

"You just caught me as I was about to go out, Mr. Styles," she said. "Really, I was a little flabbergasted by your talk on the phone. A homicide? A kidnapping? Well, come in, and let me hear what's happened to you. Someone must really have been hallucinating to you."

He hadn't paid too much attention to the living room on his first visit. He was conscious now that the pastel colors that were the keynote of the room went perfectly with her dark hair, her personal vivid coloring.

"What is this about Weldy and someone named—was it Hernandez?"

"Fernandez. Juan Fernandez," Peter said.

She perched, as she had on his first visit, on the arm of the couch, swinging an elegant leg. Her smile was bright, but relaxed. She looked anything but frightened, or even concerned. She was, he thought, for God sake, almost flirtatious.

"Let me take it from the top, Mrs. Potter," he said. "Your husband was never taken out of this country. Keach didn't fly him to Carrados. He flew a stand-in, whom neither the copilot nor the stewardess ever saw face to face."

"But they testified they saw Dick leave the plane in Carrados and walk across the airstrip," she said.

"They saw someone walk away from the plane, his back to

170

them. The copilot, Connors, had no reason to believe it wasn't your husband when Keach said 'There goes our boy.' The stewardess doubted, because she was in the habit of carrying messages from your husband to Lynn Mason. When the passenger didn't seem to understand what she was asking, through the closed door of the plane compartment, she doubted."

"So Dick had a message carrier. He's really a bad boy, you know."

"None of this would have worked," Peter said, looking at her steadily, "if Sam Evans had made the trip, as he was supposed to. We know now that he was drugged."

"Poor Sam," she said. "I haven't gotten over the news we heard last night. But drugged? I think not. Sam had a drinking problem. He took on too much the night before the trip, and tried to explain it away by saying someone had 'slipped him a Mickey.' I'm afraid that's all there is to that, Mr. Styles."

"I have located the place where it happened," Peter said. "I know exactly how much he had to drink, not enough to knock him out. I know who drugged his drink and I know that it was on instructions from Keach."

A faint frown appeared like pencil marks above her eyes. "You say you *know* this?"

"I know it, Mrs. Potter."

"And what is this about Weldy and someone named Fernandez?"

"Fernandez is a South American movie actor," Peter said.

She shrugged. "I don't like foreign films. Never look at them," she said.

"Fernandez was nearly beaten to death by someone in the Hotel Beaumont about the time Lynn Mason disappeared. He had been inquiring for me. Later on I discovered that he'd been searching my apartment. I don't know what for. He wasn't meant to survive, you understand."

171

"No, I don't understand, Mr. Styles." Her face had hard-ened, but her dark eyes were bright, like someone enjoying a dangerous game.

"Because obviously he was trying to get to me to tell me something, but he hasn't been able to talk since the beating he took. May never be able to talk. But your Mr. Keach, I think, intends to make quite certain of that. He left here less than an hour ago and went straight to Bellevue. I may just have found out in time to prevent his silencing Fernandez forever. If he made the attempt I think it's unlikely he'll be coming back here."

"Is there more to this extraordinary fairy story of yours, Mr. Styles?" She hadn't changed her relaxed position on the arm of the couch, but he thought he sensed a growing tension.

"I have identified the woman posing as your maid, your Juliana, as Lupe Vargas, a well-known revolutionary figure in Carrados. That should go a long way toward tying this whole conspiracy into the terrorists, Mrs. Potter. The only thing I'm missing is a certainty as to who is running this show. I've begun to wonder if it's you. I don't believe Keach is the man to hold it together. Is it Calvin Trevor? Is it Gabe Zorn? Is it one of the other big shots in one of the other areas of Harkness Chemical? It doesn't really matter as far as you, and Keach, and Señora Vargas are concerned. I think there is enough to make a very solid case against all three of you. And before we're done we may be able to nail you for Sam Evans's murder, too."

She leaned forward, like someone genuinely interested. "What I don't understand, Mr. Styles, is why you have come here to tell me all this. Why aren't the police, or the FBI, or the CIA with you? Why a sociable talk?"

"The possibility of plea bargaining," Peter said.

"Bargaining for what?" Frances Potter asked. She looked at Peter as if he was some kind of strange creature she didn't understand.

"The safe return of Lynn Mason and your husband," he said.

She threw back her head and actually laughed. "Oh my, Mr. Styles, you've hit so many of the outer rings on the target, but nothing near the bull's-eye. So—" and she was looking past Peter at the inner door behind him. "So we have a problem, don't we, my love?"

Peter turned. A tall, rather distinguished-looking man was standing there. He had a full beard and mustache.

"You've been a very busy little man, Styles," the bearded one said. "You don't recognize me, do you? Four months has produced a very nice natural disguise. I am Richard Potter."

The whole structure that Peter had built seemed to come tumbling down. Richard Potter, alive and well, in his own apartment, apparently under no restraint!

A second man appeared behind Potter in the doorway.

"We know he carries a gun, Wilfred," Potter said. "Take it away from him, please."

Wilfred Hadley came across the room, a police special aimed straight at Peter's heart. "You stupid sonofabitch," Hadley said, "we were doing fine until you stuck your nose into this." He took the gun out of Peter's pocket and backed away. Frances Potter hadn't moved from her relaxed position on the arm of the couch. She was enjoying herself, Peter thought. She was having a ball.

"Wilfred's right, you know," Potter said. "Until Sam Evans and you started to play little tin heroes everything was going smoothly. No one was intended to be hurt. I was sitting here in my own apartment, the last place in the world anyone would look for me. Negotiations were going smoothly; taking a long time but going smoothly. Then Sam Evans got into it. Now you. You've brought about an unfortunate blood bath between you. I hope your conscience will punish you—in the time you've got left."

173

Peter thought he had never seen colder eyes than Potter's.

"The stakes are too big, Mr. Styles, far too big," Potter said. "We couldn't let one man stand in the way—Sam Evans. You've spread out the necessities. It was a mistake to let Lynn know I was in the States, but she could have been saved if I had had time to persuade her to see things my way. Now you've left me no time, and she must be dealt with, along with you, and the stewardess who wasn't convinced, and Mamma Ortega and her little blonde whore, and your Latin American newspaper friend who must have recognized Lupe Vargas. Goddamn it, Styles, it goes on and on like a forest fire, and you started it!"

The doorbell rang in a curious sequence of rhythms. It was a signal of some sort. Frances Potter moved from the couch and went to the door. She opened it.

"Come in, Father," she said.

The Old Man, the Old Bull, came charging into the room. He pointed an angry finger at Potter. "I warned you, Dick! I warned you about this bastard." He looked at Peter, and Peter saw murder in the old eyes.

There wasn't much satisfaction in seeing this final piece of the puzzle fall into place. The Old Bull was fighting for his life, and his daughter and son-in-law were fighting on his side. He intended that at least the Carrados branch of Harkness Chemical would be his, whatever concessions he had to make to the terrorists. The young bulls weren't going to be allowed to finish him just yet.

"Thanks for coming so promptly, R.H.," Potter said. "Decisions have to be made in a hell of a hurry. Mr. Styles has come up with quite a collection of interesting facts. Put them all together and we are in what you might call a tricky situation."

"Couple of days more and we had it made," the Old Man said.

"It's a question of how much can be saved and how do we go about saving it," Potter said.

174

"There is, of course, a question we're all asking ourselves," Frances Potter said. She had crossed to a little portable bar in the corner of the living room and she brought her father a slug of something in a shot glass. The Old Man tossed it off and handed her back the glass. Frances Potter put her glass down on the table beside her. "The question is," she said, "do you have a price, Mr. Styles, and, if so, what is it?"

Peter felt like a flier coming out of an uncontrolled spin. Here was the whole story right in front of him and it didn't appear they would or could let him tell it. Potter had said it. The stakes were too big, the money, the power.

"I have a price," Peter said quietly.

"Well, what is it?" Robert Harkness demanded.

Peter ticked off the items on his fingers. "One, the safe return, unharmed, of Lynn Mason," he said. "Two, the identity of Sam Evans's murderer. Three, who assaulted, perhaps fatally, Juan Fernandez? Four—"

"Oh, for Christ sake," the Old Man said in a tone of disgust. "God save me from do-gooders! What do we do with him, Dick?"

"Whatever it is, it has to be quick," Frances Potter said. "We don't know who knows he came here, and who else knows what he knows."

"Enough people know enough to put it all together in the long run," Peter said.

"Right now it's the short run that matters," Potter said. "I think you'd better take him to the back, Wilfred."

Hadley gestured with his gun for Peter to move to the inner door. Peter had the unpleasant notion that it was probably the same gun that had eliminated Sam Evans. There was no chance for any kind of physical heroics. Potter, Hadley, and the Old Man, armed, were more than impossible odds.

The apartment was large, attractively furnished. The door through which Peter was ushered by Hadley and his gun led into a bright, sunlit hallway off which a series of rooms opened —a dining room, a library-study, and then a series of closed doors leading, Peter guessed, to bedrooms. At the very end of the hall was a door with an unusual feature to it. The Yale lock was on the outside instead of the inside. Whoever was in the room was controlled by someone on the outside. Hadley maneuvered the lock and waved Peter into the room beyond.

It was clearly a guest room; gay summer chintzes at the windows, twin beds, a door standing open revealing an empty closet. Peter watched Hadley slam the outer door shut, and heard him test it to make sure the lock had fastened properly.

"Peter!"

He turned and saw Lynn Mason. She had been stretched out on one of the beds, but was now propped up on her elbows, not really believing that it was Peter. Then she sprang to her feet and ran to him. She was suddenly clinging to him, face buried against his shoulder, weeping uncontrollably. He held her, gently, waiting. Finally she drew a deep breath and managed to choke off the tears.

"Oh, Peter, forgive me. I'm such a damned baby! But—but when I saw Hadley shove you in here my—my last hope seemed to be gone."

"Easy does it," he said. "There's an awful lot you can tell me, and perhaps some things I can tell you," Peter said. He led her back to the bed and they sat down together on the edge of it, facing each other. He held her cold hands in his, reassuring her.

"Oh God, Peter, what a nightmare!" she said.

"Now hang on and listen to me, Lynn. I walked into this not dreaming what I'd find. Potter, Hadley. I have to tell you that I don't know whether we can hope for any help in time."

"In time?"

"Between us we know too much. They're trying to decide now what to do about us. Knowing what I do about the Old Man, and his daughter, and Keach and Hadley, I don't think they'll decide to give up. And if they decide not to give up they have to decide how to get rid of us."

"Peter!" It was a whisper.

"I need to know what happened to you, Lynn. What we know is why we're in trouble, but what we know is also the only ammunition we have. What happened in the Beaumont?"

She was hanging onto him for dear life. "You—you went to speak to your friend and—and I saw him!" She shook her head from side to side. "The beard and all—but you have to understand, Peter, I—I was in love with him. I—I think I'd have known him if he'd been wearing a false face. He was—was my guy!"

"Easy, love," Peter said.

"I ran to him. He was shocked, I think. I don't think he'd seen me until I was right in front of him, reaching out to him. Then he grabbed me and literally dragged me out through a fire exit and into a sort of stairway—fire stairs, I think. We—we were both talking at once, I guess; I was saying how marvelous to see him, well and not being hampered by anyone; he saying I must stop talking and listen to him. But all he told me when I stopped talking was that—was that we must go somewhere where we *could* talk. I have to tell you, Peter, I wasn't thinking about you at all—back there in the lobby. Dick was alive, and obviously well, and there was an explanation of the marvelous fact that he was all right, not a prisoner, not—not in the kind of trouble I'd imagined. But in trouble of some sort. Of course I'd go with him—anywhere! And then—then this man with a Van Dyke beard and a mustache came through the fire door from the lobby. He seemed interested in me. 'I've been trying to find you, Miss Mason,' he said. 'I must talk to Mr. Styles.' And then he looked at Dick and he seemed suddenly shocked —frightened. I remember he said 'Potter!'—as though he couldn't believe it. And then—oh my God, Peter—Dick took a gun out of his pocket and started beating this man over the head with the butt of the gun. Not just one blow, but over and over, and I was grabbing at him, trying to stop him. Suddenly this man went somersaulting down the stairs, like—like some kind of helpless dummy—to lie sprawled out grotesquely on the floor below. 'Don't move!' Dick said, in a voice I'd never heard before—a cold, savage kind of voice. And he ran down the stairs to—oh, God, I don't know, Peter—maybe to finish off the man. I was frozen. I couldn't go anywhere, somehow. But there was a house phone right there on the landing and I—I took the receiver down and asked for you. I told the operator where you were. And I waited, and waited—watching Dick. He was bent over the man, examining him. He—he was satisfied after a few moments, I guess. He started up the stairs—and saw me at the phone. He came running toward me, telling me to put down the phone. 'Put it down!' I—I was suddenly terrified of him, terrified of the man I loved. He was someone else, someone different, someone new—and dreadful!''

"Take it slowly, Lynn. You hung up just as I was answering."

"He snatched the phone out of my hand and hung it up. He had hold of me then. 'We've got to get out of here,' he said. He started to drag me down the stairs to—to where the man lay in a pool of blood. I thought I would scream, but I couldn't make any sound come out. At the foot of the stairs I—I actually had to step over the body. Dick dragged me out through a basement exit and up onto the street. He flagged a taxi and pushed me into it. I thought of asking the driver for help, but Dick was twisting my arm, sitting there whispering to me. 'It will all make sense to you, darling, when I can tell you,' he said. 'But not here, not in the cab.' And then—then he brought me here. There is a back entrance, Peter. He didn't bring me through the lobby, the ordinary way. We came up to the fourteenth floor on the freight elevator, and he let us into the kitchen entrance with a key. This was his apartment, the place where he lived with his wife! I knew that. He brought me to this

178

room and said he'd join me in a minute and explain everything. He left. I tried to follow him and found I was locked in. There —there's no fire exit from here. From these windows it's a sheer drop of fourteen stories. I guess if there was a fire you'd have to go out into the hall and—and I don't know, Peter. There's no way out of this room and bath except through that locked door—locked on the outside."

"Did he come back? Did he explain?" Peter asked.

"I don't understand, really, what he tried to tell me," Lynn said. "Some people in Harkness Chemical were trying to push Robert Harkness out of control. Others, like Dick, and Wilfred Hadley, and Weldon Keach—and of course, Dick's wife, Frances—believe the Old Man still knows more about running the business than anyone else. Something about the politics in Carrados. I don't understand. The Old Man has believed for some time that the terrorists would take over the government there. The rest of the top people at Harkness disagree. They support the Perrault government. The Old Man saw a way to get what he wanted. They would fake the kidnapping of Dick, actually working with the terrorists. Ransom money would be paid out at once for his release, and that money would help finance the scheme. In the end, the failure to get Dick released by the imaginary kidnappers would result in the collapse of the Perrault government. The terrorists would take over and the Harkness Chemical assets in Carrados would come into the hands of the Old Man and Dick and the others. He tried to explain to me that it was good for business, that the Perrault government was corrupt, that the terrorists had the good of the people at heart, and that if—if I would just go along, when this was over, Frances would divorce him and we'd have a whole new world together."

"I think he was telling you the truth as he sees it," Peter said.

"But murder, Peter? Sam Evans was murdered. He found out something in Carrados, went to his apartment when he got

179

back, found Hadley there and accused him of being part of a conspiracy. I think Hadley killed him."

"I think so too. Did you know that before he went to his apartment Sam Evans went to your place? You weren't there."

"Why, Peter?"

"I think he was going to tell you what he believed he'd found out about your man's kidnapping."

"If I'd been there—he might not have gone—?"

"Sooner or later he would have gone, Lynn. Did Potter explain anything about the man at the Beaumont? His name is Juan Fernandez. Did he explain about him?"

She seemed exhausted from the telling. She rested her head against his shoulder. "The man was an actor, I think. They hired him to take Dick's place on the flight to Carrados. They paid him well for it, Dick said, but when the story broke in the press, about the kidnapping, the man—is it Fernandez?—tried to blackmail them for more, much more money. That day—at the Beaumont—they got word that he was there at the hotel looking for you. He was evidently going to tell you what he knew. Neither Keach nor Hadley was here at the apartment when they got the word and Dick took the chance of going after him himself. If I—if I hadn't been there and recognized him he would have gotten away with killing Fernandez without anyone dreaming—"

"Fernandez is still alive—if Keach hasn't gotten to him this morning," Peter said. "Potter didn't kill him. Not quite. Lynn, I know what this must have done to you. I know that finding out that a man you cared for—"

"I don't care for him, Peter! Do you know that he tried to make love to me—with his wife right here in the apartment—to persuade me to—to— Oh, Peter, he's not anybody I ever knew before. What is going to happen now?"

He put his arm around her, held her close. "They're going to decide to give up—or not to give up," he said. "They're all

180

headed for criminal prosecution if you and I can tell what we know. Hadley will be wanted for the murder of Sam Evans; Dick Potter for the attempted murder of Fernandez; Keach for the murder of Fernandez if he got to him this morning. All of them for conspiracy and accessories to murder or attempted murders. If they decide to give up, that's a part of what they'll face."

"And so—they won't give up?"

"I don't think so, Lynn."

"And so there is—no way?"

His arm tightened around her. "Until there is no way we have to keep thinking there is," he said.

What was it Gabriel Zorn had said? That he spent most of his time trying to think like his opposition would think. What would I do if I were in the position of Robert Harkness and the Potters? What would I do with two people who, from different perspectives, could put together a story that would totally destroy me? These people were not fools, Peter thought, unless you choose to classify all criminals as fools. There was a fanatical determination in the Old Man. There was the same fanaticism visible in the bright-faced, beautiful woman, his daughter. Potter and the others were terrorists in their own society, without conscience or heart. It wasn't hard to imagine how these people would think and act.

It would be here, Peter told himself, or they would be taken somewhere else and it would be there.

As if to answer his thought the door to the room opened and Dick Potter and Hadley came in, both holding guns. Peter and Lynn stood up, he with his arm tightly around the girl. Was it to be here?

"We can't be sure how quickly someone may come looking for you, Styles," Potter said. "We're moving now. Unfortunately both of you." He gave Lynn an almost regretful smile. "I'm sorry you couldn't see it my way, baby. It could have been

181

a very nice life, a very gay life."

Lynn turned and buried her face against Peter's shoulder again. She didn't see the bright-eyed woman in the doorway behind the two men.

"I'll never know what you ever saw in her, Dicky," she said. "A little mouse-bitch. You'll have a million better choices later on."

They were herded out into the hall. From there Peter could hear Robert Harkness talking urgently on the phone to someone. The words weren't clear as they were pushed in the opposite direction, through the apartment's kitchen and out into a service area. A freight elevator, with a bare electric light bulb burning in its ceiling, waited for them, its iron gates open. Peter and Lynn walked onto it ahead of Potter and Hadley. The gates closed, and the car started slowly down its shaft.

"I could have wished you'd had a price, Styles," Potter said. "Whatever you may think, I don't have a stomach for this. But perhaps you can see that we don't have any choice. Perhaps you can suggest something?"

Peter looked at him. He felt very tired. "I've been trying to think of some way out for you and I haven't been able to," he said. "Except, of course, when you realize that you'll be adding two murders to the charges against you, and that my editor and my friend on the homicide squad will never let up because they'll know it's you."

"On the other hand there's an outside chance they'll never be able to prove anything," Potter said. "That's the chance we'll have to take, I'm afraid. Again, Lynn, I'm sorry, dreadfully sorry. If you hadn't seen me in that hotel lobby the whole damned thing would have worked out for us in a little while." The elevator came to a halt. "There's a loading stage just beyond those sliding doors ahead of us," Potter went on. "Backed up to that stage is a panel truck. You will walk straight through the doors and into the truck. Don't make a break for it, Styles.

182

We'll just have to shoot you down and carry you away as dead meat."

They walked out of the elevator. Potter moved ahead to open the sliding doors. Hadley came behind, the barrel of his gun poked into Peter's back. Lynn was hanging onto Peter, her legs seeming to buckle under her.

A black panel truck waited at the landing stage, its rear doors closed. Potter moved quickly across the stage and opened the truck doors. He cried out a warning.

Sitting on what looked like a camp stool was Gabriel Zorn, a very efficient-looking machine pistol at the ready. For an instant Peter looked at the grinning Zorn and thought he had a final question answered. Then Zorn spoke.

"End of the line, gentlemen," he said. "Drop the guns."

The reaction was quick. Potter ducked down and backed away. Hadley gave Peter a violent shove that sent him stumbling toward Zorn in the doorway of the truck. Zorn sidestepped like a ballet dancer and the machine pistol chattered. Hadley spun around and fell.

"Drop your gun, Dicky boy," Zorn said. "I'd hate to have to give you the same treatment. I can cut you in half with this, friend." His smile broadened as Potter dropped his gun. "I would have hated to be deprived of the spectacle of you standing trial in court before the whole world, Dicky—you louse."

"Aren't you going to do something for him?" Potter asked, nodding toward Hadley.

"It would save the State a lot of money if I just let him bleed to death," Zorn said. "But, I suppose—" He reached in his vest pocket, took out a police whistle, and blew a shrill blast on it. Men came out of the shadows. "Let's go upstairs and see how that wing of the party is doing," Zorn said. "You first, Dicky boy, so I can keep an eye on you." He grinned at Peter. "As a good newspaperman I think you and Miss Mason should join us, Styles. Of course you're free to go your own way. But your

183

first ten drinks are on me, pal. I owe you."

Lynn looked at Peter, bewildered. She had no idea who Zorn was, of course. With that machine pistol he looked more like a cop than a banker.

The freight elevator wheezed up fourteen floors and stopped. A strange man was standing outside the open door of the kitchen to 14 B.

"Everything go smoothly?" Zorn asked.

"Laughable," the man said.

Zorn grinned at Peter again. "Maybe you better bring up the rear," he said. "I'd like to make an entrance with my prisoner. First time I've ever been deputized by the city police. Make the most of it!"

He walked down the hall, machine pistol at Richard Potter's back, to the living room. "You sent me the prize pigeon," he called out to someone in the room beyond.

Then Peter felt a great surge of relief sweep over him. He wanted to laugh. Instead he turned Lynn Mason around and kissed her.

"It seems I'll be able to take you out to dinner after all," he said.

Lieutenant Maxvil, wearing a cat-and-canary smile, surrounded by three obvious cops, presided over a grim little band of prisoners. Robert Harkness, Frances Potter, and Weldon Keach were all wearing handcuffs. There was a clicking noise as a fourth pair were snapped over Richard Potter's wrists. The Old Bull and his supporters had lost the game, it seemed.

"On the house," Gabriel Zorn said, as he raised his glass.

Peter and Lynn, along with Maxvil and Calvin Trevor, were on the penthouse garden at the top of the Harkness Chemical Building, shielded from the afternoon sunshine under bright beach umbrellas. Drinks had been made and served by the

184

white-coated houseman Peter had seen there on his previous visit.

"The reason you couldn't reach me," Maxvil was explaining to Peter, "was that I was waiting at Bellevue for somebody to make a try at Fernandez. Your friend Bill Duncan almost spoiled it in his effort to stop Keach, but I managed to drag him away and let Keach make his move. The bandaged man in the intensive care unit was a homicide detective. We'd moved Fernandez early this morning and set the trap. I figured someone would try to make sure he never talked."

"But how did you get to the apartment?" Peter asked.

"Duncan told me where you were. I went looking for you."

"And I was wandering around the neighborhood, waiting for you to show," Zorn said. "Told you, didn't I, I try to think like other people. When Maxvil told me about Keach, we decided you'd probably thought you could handle Mrs. Potter."

"Two and two," Maxvil said. "I had enough bragging from Keach to be certain the lady wasn't alone. We figured they'd move to prepare a quiet little execution for you and Miss Mason. Hoping we weren't too late—" Maxvil chuckled. "Zorn took the back way out with his people, saw Hadley getting that panel truck into place, and was waiting. I let myself in the front door with my people, using Keach's key. Like rolling off a log. Our friends were caught with their mouths hanging open."

Peter shook his head. "You had this lined up all along yet you sent me to do your work for you," he said to Zorn.

The big security man grinned. "People don't like to talk to cop types. No matter how hard I try people always spot me for a cop. I couldn't ask you to play along with me. You didn't trust me. But I know how to tail people. You were followed to the airport and watched. You were watched at your apartment when the stewardess brought you Santos, the newspaper guy. You were watched at Mamma Ortega's. You were watched

185

when you went back there this morning. I could almost read your mind, Styles, just watching your actions. I was about to go up to the apartment when you'd been there for a while. Too risky to let you be there long. Fortunately Lieutenant Maxvil came along and we knew, from what Keach had confessed, how dangerous it really was. So we set the trap and moved in. But we owe you, Styles. If you hadn't been able to follow the trail so expertly, we'd still be fumbling around in the dark."

"Fernandez," Peter said. "I still don't understand why he was looking for me at the Beaumont or why he searched my apartment, if he did."

"Oh, he did," Maxvil said. "What Potter told Miss Mason was true enough. Fernandez was hired to impersonate Potter on the flight to Carrados. He saw how big a deal it was when the kidnapping broke in the press, and he decided to ask for a bigger payoff. He was turned down. One of the mistakes they made. He went looking for Lynn Mason. Her story about the code message attracted him. She might help him expose the fraud. He caught up with you, Miss Mason, at the night spot where you sing. Peter was there that night, and Fernandez followed you when you left the place, thinking Peter was taking you home. Actually you came on the fire. Fernandez stayed close, heard you give names and information to the fire chief. Peter could be much more helpful than Miss Mason—if he somehow wasn't connected with Harkness Chemical. Fernandez decided to make sure, searched your apartment, found nothing to frighten him off. Then he went back to Miss Mason's —thinking, if you'll forgive me, that Peter might have spent the night there. Peter hadn't, but he came back there and took Miss Mason off with him—to the Beaumont to see Walter Franklin. The rest ties up, I guess."

"Señora Vargas?" Peter asked.

"The one that got away," Maxvil said. "Too smart for your friend Santos."

186

Zorn was enjoying himself. He took a second drink from the houseman. "I'm suggesting to Mr. Trevor, Styles, that he put you on the Harkness payroll. We could make you a lot richer than *Newsview* does."

"We are grateful," Trevor said. "We were very close here to being shaken to our foundations."

"Thanks, but I like it the way it is," Peter said. He smiled at Lynn. "If it wasn't for Miss Mason I wouldn't have been in this at all. I'm sorry it turned out for her the way it did."

Lynn smiled back at him. "It's as though I never knew him, Peter. As though Richard Potter never existed."

"It seems we never knew him either, Miss Mason," Trevor said.

Gabriel Zorn chuckled. "Like a lot of people I know, he got too big for his britches. So—drink up, friends. Tomorrow we'll be too busy to remember today."